BRENNAN

LUCKY IRISH SERIES 3

ANNA CASTOR

ANNA CASTOR

Editing: Burgeon Design and Editorial

Cover design: Anna Castor

ISBN: 9789083046235

�֍ Created with Vellum

INTRODUCTION TO LUCKY IRISH FAMILIES

F amilies in book 1 - 2:

Additional families from book 3:

Additional families from book 4:

"You know how the game works, Errin." Theresa chuckled on the other end of the line. "It's a big deal when they even give you feedback. It means they think you're worthy of a response. You should be proud."

Errin was fuming at Theresa's chuckling voice and said, "Proud? About some asswipe calling my agent to tell her I'm an uncoordinated rhino on stage?"

Errin looked over her shoulder at some old lady standing next to her on the sidewalk, clucking her tongue at her, irritated by Errin's loud voice.

"Don't shoot the messenger. I'm—"

"Yeah, yeah. I know. Sorry, Therees."

Errin stood on the edge of the street, the light October breeze warm enough for her to wear her white button-down shirt and her light blue boyfriend jeans. She crossed the street, leaving the scrutinizing old bat at the sidewalk, waiting for the light to turn green. Somewhere in the background Theresa brought up the whole 'closing a door, opening a window'-cliché, but she didn't respond. After a few obligatory "Hm-hmm's." from Errin, they hung up.

She took a right to go to her all-time favorite spot in Austin, passing the picturesque banks of Barton Springs where people picnicked on blankets in the sun with family and friends. Errin grinned at a teenage girl pushing a boy on a tube in Barton Creek before she jumped right after him into the water.

After spending some time at the outdoor theatre in Zilker Park, she took the bus back downtown. She took her time strolling on the sidewalk. She wasn't ready to go back to her empty apartment. This Saturday was her birthday and the last day of October. She would celebrate all dressed up for the Halloween party at her sisters' boyfriend's Irish pub. A vibration in her jean pocket interrupted her thoughts about sexy but cute outfits to wear. A text from her brother.

CONNER: And? Can I clear out my spare room already?

Errin smiled.

ERRIN: Nope. Didn't get the part. Not even the understudy.

CONNER: That sucks ass.

Errin didn't respond right away. It did suck. She puffed out her cheeks.

CONNER: Sorry sis.

She let out an enormous sigh and walked over at a bench next to a small park. She crossed her feet and typed back.

ERRIN: Do you know what else sucks ass?

CONNER: That we're still thousands of miles apart and can't get sloshed?

No matter how down she'd felt in these past months apart, her brother still brought out a smile from her.

ERRIN: Besides the obvious.

CONNER: Okay. I'll bite...

ERRIN: I don't know if I even want to try again.

CONNER: stfu

Errin looked up from her phone, tilted her head back and gazed over the tall building before her. She followed some bird's flutter in between rooftops and took a moment to let the rays of sunlight warm her face. After two deep breaths, she answered him.

ERRIN: No, I mean it, Con. I'm so over the whole going back and forth between here and New Jersey. Only to get zero call backs.

Her brother replied without missing a beat.

CONNER: Never took my youngest sis for a quitter.

She sniffed and shifted in her seat. Her fingers worked her phone vigorously as she typed.

ERRIN: I can get rejected over here anytime. Believe me. No need to get on a plane to hear from some NY schmuck that I need to work on my frame and lose 10 pounds.

The words of the casting director still baffled her. The audacity of that jerk. No, she wasn't a teenager anymore, and keeping in shape hadn't been as easy as years ago. But she'd danced most of her life and she was a lean but strong five foot five. She wasn't ashamed of her body and wouldn't let some random stranger tell her otherwise. At twenty-five, she knew exactly where he could stick his *feedback*.

CONNER: Fuck them. You know you can come back home without the whole dancing shit?

Before she could reply, he continued typing.

CONNER: I mean it. Stay with me, sis. Or stay at mom and dad's. We all want you back home.

Tears trailed over her cheek, and she wiped them away. Pff. There she was, crying all alone on a worse for wear bench near some stinking city park. But leave it to Conner to go in for the kill.

CONNER: If it wasn't for our sisters settling down south, we'd have hauled all yer arses back a long time ago.

Only when worked up enough, he'd let his Irish brogue out. Even via text. Errin gave a watery smile and replied.

ERRIN: I know. But just like I miss you guys back home, I would miss Kayla and Kate here too. I might as well keep trying to get a gig here.

CONNER: Hm.

She'd followed her sister Kayla to Austin last April after Kayla survived an attack by some psycho co-worker. While Kayla was lying in a hospital bed, Errin and Kate promised they'd move to Austin so the three sisters would be together again. She wasn't going back on their pact just because she was homesick. Now, if she'd landed a big role in New Jersey, it would be a whole different story. She was sure that Kayla would even help her pack her bags so she could follow her dreams.

Errin glanced up from her phone and laughed at the sign on the building across the street.

She snapped a picture of the business, grinning. 'Pawty Hard.' She texted Conner..

ERRIN: Let me send you a pic real quick...

She zoomed in on the 'help wanted' sign in the dog kennel's window. She might as well have a look inside, even though she hated dogs with a passion. Okay, she was scared shitless of the barking and biting mongrels. But her latest trip back home reduced her savings to nil, so beggars couldn't be choosers. Right? Her phone vibrated.

CONNER: A man, his son, and a dog walk into a bar...

ERRIN: ?

CONNER: "Ow" "Ow" "Whoof"

She snickered.

ERRIN: Dork.

CONNER: Talk later? I'm with Evan, having a beer at Calum's.

A pang of jealousy stabbed her stomach at the mention of her three brothers sitting together, having beers and talking shit.

ERRIN: Say hi for me, will you?

CONNER: Will do. Keep ya chin up, okay? Talk later.

CONNER: Or is it chins up? Since you need to lose 10 pounds?

ERRIN: Fuck off

CONNER: Whaha love you sis.

ERRIN: hm

She paused, thinking of her goofy brother.

ERRIN: Love you, too

B rennan looked over the worn oak bar at Ed, a regular. He showed up tonight in a ridiculous horse suit and sat hunched over his dark ale.

Next to Ed leaned Brennan's youngest brother, Ronan, dressed as Hugh Hefner. Already drunk halfway through the night, but somehow he still signaled for another round.

"Last one. Take it easy, bro," Brennan said while walking over to the tap and glancing over his shoulder as a half-dressed nurse and stewardess fell off of their bar stools. Their Halloween costumes were almost as over the top as their cackles on their way to the floor.

"Yo, Dec!" Brennan shouted over the music to his other brother dressed as Batman. He jerked his chin at the women.

"I've got them," Declan said. He steadied the women as they flopped around like fish and escorted them towards the exit. The scantily clad nurse pouted over her shoulder at Brennan and whined, "Aww, can't we stay with you tonight?"

"Nope."

He wasn't in the habit of taking patrons upstairs to his two-bedroom apartment above his family's Irish pub, The Lucky Irishman. And he wouldn't make an exception for her. He was nothing like his old man, who for sure would have taken her up on her offer.

Sean Jr., his father, walked in through the swinging doors from the kitchen with an enormous birthday cake for Errin. Brennan strode to the sound system to switch songs while Errin's brothers walked in behind Sean Jr. singing 'Happy Birthday' while popping confetti all over the place.

Yeah, fuckin' great. Some time around Fourth of July he would still find those motherfuckers in a glass of wine somewhere. He searched for Bunny, as her family nicknamed Errin after the Energizer Bunny.

She danced on top of a chair, her body curving to the upbeat music. When the rest of the pub started singing along, Errin jumped off the chair on a high-pitched squeal and ran like her arse was on fire.

"I can't believe it! You're really here!" she shrieked. Her brothers had surprised her by flying in from New Jersey.

She jumped into the arms of her oldest brother, Calum, and the rest of the Walshes joined in on the reunion huddle. She hiccupped while crying and clung to them like it was the last time she'd ever hug them again.

But Brennan wasn't mistaken. His brother Duncan had described Errin as an 'angelic spitfire' after first meeting her. Under her sweet and innocent shell lurks a girl who swears like a sailor and talks before she thinks.

She even sets his brother Ronan in his place with confrontational conversations and stupid jokes. A slight smile tugged his upper lip, and he shook his head.

About an hour later, he leaned in over the bar to decipher another slurred order. "And one Ssseaa Breeezz."

He nodded at the guy and picked up his credit card from the oak bar. Errin caught his eye when her fine arse sashayed through the pub and stopped four barstools over to order.

His coworkers Tori and Jessica were in charge of that side of the bar. He ignored Errin while she swayed to the music with her eyes closed, singing along with the music.

She had surprised him tonight by turning up in a cute black ballerina outfit instead of some overly sexy costume. Her long honey colored braid kept sliding over her right breast, grazing her nipple repeatedly and making it stand out like a sore thumb against the shiny fabric of her outfit. But he wasn't going there. *Hell no.*

She wasn't his type.

Sure, Errin was hot. A professional dancer with a body to show for it, and not to mention those beautiful aquamarine doe eyes and long, warm blonde hair. But that mouth on her? Within the first thirty seconds in meeting her, he concluded they would never be a thing. Or even friends.

"Hi Tori. Can you get me a round of tequila shots?" Errin shouted over the pumping music. "And do one with me!" Brennan looked at that luscious but loud mouth that never stopped talking. Often yapping about stupid things he didn't have the time for. Stupid things he wasn't even remotely interested in.

He guessed their eleven-year age difference made it so he couldn't relate to her half of the time. Or perhaps it was for the lack of trying.

He's determined to stay away from that cluster fuck. She was the youngest Walsh sister, and he wasn't about to get involved with the sister of Kayla and Kate.

They might date his brothers Duncan and Donovan, but the Walsh-Mills connection would end right there. It would get messy the moment things would end between him and Errin. Probably sooner.

Tori walked over to his side of the bar to grab the tequila bottle and caught him staring at Errin.

"Pfff. Black Swan... thinks she owns the place..." Tori muttered under her breath.

"What's that?" Brennan said as he walked by to grab the ice bucket near Tori's feet under the sink. They were almost out of ice and he needed to fill this spare bucket.

"Hmm?" she asked like she hadn't heard him.

He had no time for this and left Tori standing there. While he was filling the ice bucket, Tori passed him to stand behind the register where she handed over the pin device to Errin.

Errin pulled her cellphone from her outfit where it rested over her breast. She took her card from her phone case and placed it in the pin device. Tori was making Errin pay for her drinks, even though he'd instructed the staff that Errin's drinks were on the house tonight since it was her birthday.

He stepped up and snatched the pin device out of Errin's hands before she'd confirm her payment.

"What the fuck?" Errin said. Her narrowed eyes met his and in their stand-off, she ignored his outstretched hand to return her card. He raised a brow, and she shook her head.

"Drinks are on the house, Errin. Happy birthday," he said.

She leaned over the bar, giving him a perfect view of those handfuls pushing against the bodice of her outfit. "So if I would ring this old sailor's bell above my head, you'd pay for those drinks too?" She smiled like the cat that got the cream.

He wasn't one to go back on his word, but fuck. It would seriously hurt to give the whole pub a round during a full house on Halloween. Errin crooked her finger for him to lean in from his side of the bar.

"I'm just messing with you, Brennan Mills. Thanks for the drinks," she said and smacked a kiss on his cheek. She winked and left him leaning over the bar, eyes following her lithe body as she maneuvered through the throng of people, a tray of shots held high above her head. He traced her kiss on his cheek with his thumb.

Ed signaled for another dark ale.

"Yeah, yeah... I'll get you another."

The night passed quickly and hours later, after he'd set the last of the glasses in the two industrial sized dishwashers in the kitchen, he reentered the pub.

Errin still sat with Pops at his table, head resting on top of her arms, draped over the table top.. Yes, his grandfather has his own table and when he'd entered the place, they expected people to move from his spot. The former owner of Lucky and patriarch of the Mills family sure had his perks.

Brennan stepped behind the bar to work on the numbers and stats from the cash register. He couldn't concentrate with those two sitting nearby. Pops said he'd liked the Irish fire coming from Errin and because the two of them never beat around any bush, they just clicked.

Pops patted her messy braided hair, leaned in and said, "Dear lass. Nothin' bad about workin' at a dog kennel. Even if ye hate dogs. Do ye think I always knew what I was doin' with me life?" He chuckled as he nudged her shoulder with his knuckles.

She groaned.

"Ye are the worst drunk I've ever seen in me life. Ha! And I've run an Irish Pub throughout the sixties, seventies and eighties."

Errin giggled and snorted. "I don't believe you, old man. No way I'm the worst."

Brennan raised his brows. Nobody from his family would ever dare to call Pops an old man, but Pops let her get away with almost anything.

"Who ye callin' an old man? Anyway, I ain't listenin' to nobody who's named after a rodent."

Errin lifted her head from her hands and glowered at him. "Who are you calling a rodent?"

"Well, ain't people callin' ye Bunny?"

Errin busted out in laughter and even drowned out Pop's bellowing laugh. When Brennan joined them, Errin and Pops looked up.

Errin stabbed some tears from her cheeks. Were those tears of joy or had she been emotional because she couldn't hold her liquor?

Errin could get drunk from sniffing a stale beer bottle. He'd been on the front-row seat of her drunken laughter one too many times. And she *never* listened to him when he would try to cut her off after three drinks.

Yep, it took two drinks for Errin to slur. *Shit.* How was she getting home tonight? Her brothers left with Kayla for an after party at her and Duncan's house, leaving her the last Walsh. Brennan often let Pops stay in his spare room upstairs whenever he would be the last one to leave—like tonight. But what was he going to do with Errin?

As his eyes met Pops', he stood and patted Errin's hair.

"Imma goin' crash in ye spare room tonight, boyo." Brennan nodded at Pops. "Lass, let me boyo take care of ye, okay? And don't give 'em any lip, ye hear?"

Errin snorted and her eyes drifted over from Pops to lock with Brennan's. "He would love to have a nibble, but he isn't getting my lips, Pops. I promise." She pouted those big puffy lips in a fake kiss and winked at Brennan, the wench.

"Irish fire, I'll tell ye. Brennan, me boy, watch out for me dear lass. Just when ye think ye safe, she's gonna fire it all up. Bringin' ye walls down."

"Pops..."

But Pops was already walking through the backdoor and heading up to Brennan's apartment. And now it was just the two of them.

Brennan had already stopped the music and flicked on the lights. He'd swept and cleaned most of the tables. One last table to go.

He closed the register and picked up his towel, a sponge, and cleaning solution. The checkout had to wait till tomorrow. He strode to Pops' table where Errin still sat.

Errin eyed him with mascara trails running down her cheeks like she was seeing him for the very first time. *Oh, hell no.* She had to stop giving him the look.

The look that said she was game for the night. The look that said she wanted to forget whatever's been bothering her, and he was the number one solution to make her forget. She wasn't the first woman who'd eyed him like this at closing time in Lucky.

He sprayed the cleaning formula on the table and wiped it over and over with his sponge. Her penetrating gaze followed his every move, but he intended to keep on ignoring her.

He would not give in to her sudden interest in him. She showed none before, so why now—because she was drunk? That had to be the number one turnoff for him. How cliché of her.

"So..." she said.

He spared a glance over his shoulder at Errin sitting at the table, and sure enough, she blushed the moment their eyes met. Fuck. Errin never blushed.

"Stop it," he warned.

Her light blue eyes grew wide, and she stuttered, "S-stop w-what?"

"Stop staring at me." He lifted one eyebrow and dared her to contradict him.

"I—"

"Stop looking at me as if you want me to pick you up, throw you on this table and fuck the life out of you," he said and returned his focus on his hands that kept assaulting the tabletop with his sponge. *Damn confetti.*

Errin gasped. "Oh-my-god! Are you serious?"

"That's what you've been thinking about, isn't it?" he stopped scrubbing and glanced over his shoulder again.

Her wide eyes ping-ponged from the tabletop to his face again. "I... erm, no! Never. *You* stop it. I have no idea what's going on inside that head of *yours,* but I'll have you know that nobody will ever throw me over any kind of surface to get fucked. And certainly not you! Ugh."

She was such a terrible liar. Her cheeks reddened even more and her eyes blazed with fire. Those beautiful baby blues were shooting daggers at him and the weird thing was, it was making him hard as hell. He didn't want her, but fuck if his body didn't get that memo.

To derail their inescapable route to 'FuckedupVille', he wanted to get her out of his pub as soon as possible. Otherwise he couldn't be held responsible for his actions. "Okay, so I'll take you upstairs."

"W-what? No. I wanna go home." She pouted those damn glossy lips again while wiping the messy mascara trails from under her eyes.

"Why are you talking like a five-year-old?" he muttered, giving the table a few last scrubs.

"Am not!" she sulked, crossing her arms in front of her chest, drawing his eyes to the little swell that now peeked over the bodice of her leotard.

The cute pout she wore made her fuckin' adorable where he often found other women annoying. But not Errin. She always spoke her mind, often brutally honest, and would never play the innocent pouty type to gain his attention. Thinking about Errin's feisty attitude, his face turned up.

She tilted her head while assessing him. "Why don't you ever smile? You—"

"I'm taking the couch, so you can take the second bedroom to your left. Otherwise you'll be sleeping next to a heavily snoring Pops. And let me tell you, that shit ain't pretty."

Her face reddened. "Stop talking to me like I'm a kid! I turned twenty-six today, you know. You don't get to—"

"Errin, go upstairs and stop looking for a fight. You're not supposed to give me any lip, remember?"

He examined her plump lips. She'd put some glossy shit on, making them even more pink than usual. She licked her lips, evoking a groan from him.

"What?" she said as she tucked an unruly strand of warm blond hair behind her ear, only to have it pop up again in the next second.

"Stop teasing me," he said.

"I'm not teasing you, old man. Never. I'm not interested. I'm nothing like your normal bimbo-type that throw themselves at you."

He narrowed his eyes at her. But she didn't stop there, no.

"What do they see in you, anyway? I mean... you're always so... angry? Huh, and dare I say boring? And let's not forget self-righteous? Ha! I mean the way you—"

Just to shut her the hell up, he kissed her. His hand slid to the back of her head the moment he'd dropped the wet sponge onto the table. She moaned against his lips but didn't open up for him. He grabbed her tiny waist with his other hand and pulled her up from the chair.

She gasped when his erection pressed against her belly and he slid his tongue in her mouth and let his tongue play with hers. They stood in the middle of the pub, flooded by the harsh overhead lights and surrounded by the smell of stale beer. As they kissed, everything faded to the background, as if they stood somewhere else.

The gurgling sound from the running fridge reminded him he was standing in the middle of Lucky kissing Errin. He pulled his face away and took a step back. He wiped his mouth with the back of his hand.

"Second door to your left."

L oud snoring woke her up in the middle of the night. An earsplitting headache threatened to pulverize her brain.

She tried to guess which room she was in, but as it was pitch black, nothing stood out. She padded the mattress next to her and it came up cold and empty.

Her hand traveled the mattress in the other direction and her phone's screen lit up at the touch. Now that she had a bit of light, she reached for the bedside lamp so she could absorb her surroundings. The first thing that caught her eye was the king-size bed stuffed in a room too small to house such enormous bed.

She figured this must be Brennan's room. On the dresser sat a golden picture frame with a picture of a little Brennan hugged by a woman with ebony hair falling down over her shoulders.

The attractive woman wore plastic purple earrings that matched her dress. They both had the same light green eye color, olive skin and black hair. Errin was sure this woman was his deceased mother.

Why, oh why, had she drank so much last night? Halloween... Birthday cake... Her brothers who flew in to surprise her... Kissing Brennan....

Back up... *Kissing Brennan?* She shot up in bed but wished

she hadn't. She groaned at the piercing pain inside her brain. Nooo, she kissed him? Hmm, come to think of it. *He* kissed *her. Ha, that old fox, eh?*

And he never once gave her the least bit of attention these past months. *Huh.* She never took the time to let her mind go there with him. Sure, he wasn't hard to look at. Okay—breathtakingly beautiful in a dark and moody way was more descriptive of his looks.

But Errin had been around the block. She could spot an emotionally detached bachelor from a mile away. And Brennan had it written all over that handsome, worry lined face of his. Not to mention that as a Mills brother, he was sort of family now since both of her sisters had paired up with two of his four brothers.

She lifted the comforter and was happy to find her leotard and tutu still intact. Her ballet slippers were in a pool of white-laced ribbon next to the bed, but she didn't have time to put on her shoes and tie the ribbon around her calves. She needed to get out of here. Now.

What happened last night, hmm just hours ago, had been a mistake. A glance at her phone told her it was five in the morning. She checked if her cards and key were in her phone case. She opened the flash light app on her phone and turned off the bedside lamp.

Her pedicured black painted toenails showed in the harsh and tunneled light. She tilted her phone and spotted a door. Next up was grabbing her shoes before tiptoeing around the room. When the snoring from the other room continued, she took a few pensive steps.

She pushed the door, and it creaked open. She cringed at the sound. The snoring grew louder, and she grinned. Brennan must have been used to it, as he often let Pops crash in his apartment.

She opened the door to the stairs leading down to the pub when a rough hand grabbed her shoulder.

"What the fuck?" roared a deep voice behind her.

She gasped and almost shit herself in angst. She stumbled backwards, and the room tilted upside down as she careened down the stairs. Her head hit the wall.

"Ouch. That hurts," she said, rubbing her head.

"Errin! Fuck!" Brennan shouted. He reached down with rough hands and picked her up. He held her close to his warm body, the scent of sandalwood engulfing her.

"Come," he whispered in her hair.

She leaned in and sniffed behind Brennan's ear. He smelled so damn nice. He tensed and cleared his throat.

"Ye fuckin' scared me half to death. What were ye even thinkin' of doin' out there?"

Brennan's reprimanding and stern voice brought her out of her haze. The Mills brothers only threw out the Irish sounding 'ye's' when pissed off.

Well, she'd show him pissed off.

"I wanted to bump and grind your stairway, asshole. What else did you think I wanted to do?"

He walked them back into the apartment that was flooded in light.

"What's all that ruckus about? Boyo!"

Pops stood halfway in the spare bedroom's doorway in red plaid pajamas with his hand still on the light switch in the living room. His gray hair pointed in all directions and he eyed them. Oh, how she loved that massive grumpy bear.

"It was nothing. Go back to bed, Pops."

"Don't ye tell yer grandfather to go back to bed, ye brat. I'll tell ye, I might be old, but you'll never send me away like a damn child. Ye hear?"

"I'm sorry, Pops." Brennan sighed and his warm breath

tickled Errin's neck, making her shudder. He tightened his grip on her. "She just scared the ever living shit out of me."

"Ahh, if that ain't me dear lass," Pops said, eyes gleaming. "Will ye look at that? Now, ain't youse two a sight for sore eyes?"

Errin squeaked when Brennan almost let her slip out of his hands.

"Okay, Pops. Let it go."

"Aye, boyo. I'll let youse alone. Give youse some private time, eh?" Pops' smiling face was infectious, making Errin grin.

"Pops—" But Pops held up his big calloused hand and shut the door behind him. Pops put on some old Frank Sinatra song and when the first frolic tunes of 'I've Got You Under My Skin' started, Brennan snorted.

"Shit. The older he gets, the more—"

"I love Pops. He's the best. He's the only one who can handle me and my big mouth," Errin folded her arms over her chest and jutted her chin at him.

Brennan guffawed, his inky hair falling over his eyes as he glanced down at her in his arms. "Oh, I can handle you just fine."

She rolled her eyes before she narrowed them at him. "Will you just set me down already?"

He walked them over to his worn but comfy looking brown couch. He sat her down, the spot on the couch underneath her bum still warm where he'd just been sleeping. "So. What do we have here?" he said before he took a seat on the edge of the low coffee table in front of her.

He wasn't wearing a shirt, just a pair of worn gray sweatpants. His strong pecs distracted her enough to not wince from her pain as he trailed a finger over her hurt ankle.

Hair covered his chest, making him somehow even manlier. If she leaned in just a teeny bit, she could suck on his pointy nipple. Was he aroused or just cold? He knelt before her just in time before she did something stupid.

"Let me have a closer look."

He picked up her left leg and a sharp pain stung in her ankle. "Ouch! That hurts, ass—"

"Well, at least that big mouth of yours still works." He smirked.

"It takes a lot more than some bastard stairs to shut me up."

He chuckled and shook his head. She narrowed her eyes. "You're so full of yourself. I mean, it ain't even funny."

"You know, Bunny... I have my ways to shut you up. It worked just fine last night, so if you don't stop running your mouth, I'm—"

"Oh, for fuck's sake. Don't tell me you kissed me because you wanted me to shut up. How old are you? Like twelve? Can't even admit that—"

And then he kissed her.

Again.

But oh, this time it was an even angrier kiss than before. He grabbed the back of her head to hold her in place as he set the pace, growling into her open mouth. She loved the way he took control of the kiss. And even her.

His other hand traveled up from her calf to her thigh and halted at her hip. She placed her hand on his chest, familiarizing her fingers with his chest hair.

He grabbed her toned waist and scooted her to the edge of the couch. She slid her leg around his waist and her ankle smarted, sending a jolt of pain through her foot.

"Aaah. Fuck. That hurts," she cried.

"I don't want to interrupt ye party, but I also don't want to listen to an entire CD of Frank at five in the mornin'. Can yous two tone down ye Irish fire?" Pops bellowed.

Errin's eyes grew wide at Brennan's tanned but now flushed

skin. She laughed a full on belly laugh, glancing at Brennan—a scolded schoolboy, bobbing his Adam's apple and searching for a place behind her to fixate his eyes on. Her foot slipped from behind Brennan's back to the ground, and she cried out again.

His green eyes were kind as he placed her foot on his strong muscular thigh to examine it. His thumb stroked her swollen ankle. "I'm taking you to the hospital, Lips."

She bristled and tried to pull away from him, but he held her firmly in place with his hand on her hip.

"What the hell are you calling me?"

"Exactly..."

"Never mind. I'm calling Calum. He's staying at my apartment tonight. He can take me." She searched for her phone next to her on the couch. Brennan cleared his throat and waved her phone at her. Sneaky bastard.

"Your brother is sleeping. Let me take you. I'm already up." He shrugged like it was no skin off his back.

With an annoyed huff, she held out her hand to him, palm up. He gave her a lopsided grin and with a rather flair for drama, dropped her phone into her palm.

"Thanks."

"Let me grab a shirt before I take you." He stood and rested her foot on his deserted spot on the coffee table. His cockiness about taking her to the ER no matter what she would counter was irritating as hell, but even Errin had to agree that calling her overbearing brother at five in the morning wasn't the best plan. Dodging Calum's questions about her staying over at Brennan and getting injured was a much better option.

He returned in a gray washed T-shirt that stretched over his chest and black jeans that clung to his tree trunk thighs. She whirled around but startled when he appeared in front of her and picked her up in one swift move. She held her tongue about his alpha ways, but his chuckles told her she wasn't fooling him by giving him the silent treatment.

"You really hate this, eh Lips?"

"Whatever," she muttered. "Just take me to the ER."

She kept her gaze fixed on his Adam's apple. Her eyes traveled over his five o'clock shadow to his chiseled chin, and she fought back the urge to run her nails through the prickly hairs.

He walked her down the stairs into the pub and through the back door. Outside, he walked in a straight line to his black truck, parked in the now deserted and dimly lit parking lot behind Lucky.

He cradled her in one arm and opened the passenger door with the other. He set her on the seat, his manly sandalwood scent wafting over her. She closed her eyes and inhaled as he clicked her seatbelt for her. When she opened her eyes, his striking light green eyes locked on hers.

"Peas..." he whispered.

"What?"

"Forgot to take you through the kitchen to pick up a bag of frozen peas for your ankle. I'll be right back." He turned to run back inside.

"Don't leave me here all alone at five in the morning with the car doors open!".

He came to a stop, turned and ran back.

"Shit. Sorry. Didn't mean to leave you like that. Although, I don't think there is anyone in the entire state of Texas willing to kidnap your bitchy arse and get you out of my hands."

He winked as he closed the door and locked it with the button on his key fob. He tapped the window twice with his knuckles and she flipped him the bird. He laughed.

His messy hair, that only ever seemed to be combed by his fingers, grazed his forehead as he shook his head.

"Okay. Go."

Brennan's chortle at her swift shooing motions gave her a warm feeling deep inside. She sighed as her eyes followed his retreating muscular back. He had her so distracted that only now, as she sat alone with her swollen ankle, she wondered what this injury would mean to her dancing career.

"Shit," she whispered.

Austin

Brennan
4

"You can put me down now. I'm sure I can walk the short distance to my apartment."

He glanced down at her small hand resting on his chest, urging him to set her down, and arched his brow for the fiftieth time that night-slash-morning. Who would have thought you could take your pick of any Mills man and Errin would still be more pig-headed?

It relieved him to know the bump on her head proved to be nothing serious. But the doctor said she'd mildly sprained her ankle and needed to let it rest for at least a week. He put her down, and she hopped a few wobbly steps on crutches before she almost slipped and fell. He swooped her up again and kept on walking undeterred through the hallway, although she wriggled her tiny firm butt in his arms in protest.

"Number?"

"404."

Before he could ask her for the key, the door opened and Errin's brother Calum appeared in the doorway in his dark blue pajama bottoms.

Calum slid a hand through his silver blonde hair before he crossed his arms in front of his broad bare chest and blocking their path. "What in the hell is going on here?"

"She needs to rest and elevate her ankle. Step aside."

Brennan was no man for drama. Big brother dearest, who no doubt wanted to warn Brennan off from his sister, didn't bother him. There was no need for that pissing match. He was not interested, so why partake in that whole song and dance?

"What do you mean? What happened?" Calum asked as he took a slight step aside. Before Brennan passed him, Calum grabbed Errin out of his arms.

"I can walk just fine, Cal. Just let me—"

Calum interrupted her, "No, Bunny. Dunno what happened, but you're going to bed, like it or not."

Errin replied by blowing away the few escaped honey strands from her braid out of her face. She made a big show out of her annoyance, and Brennan just suppressed a smirk. He followed the siblings into what had to be Errin's bedroom and placed her crutches against the nightstand.

He never thought he'd ever step a foot inside her place, let alone her bedroom. As he expected, it wasn't filled with flowery, girly shit.

A queen-sized bed dominated the room, and above the headboard was a poster of a silhouetted couple dancing, their bodies captured in contorted angles.

On her nightstand stood a photograph of Errin sandwiched in a bear hug with Calum and Conner. It took no effort to imagine her signature loud laugh as he looked twice at the picture.

Since he was here, Brennan figured he'd make sure she'd be okay. He pulled away the purple comforter, and Calum placed her in the middle of the bed. Brennan spotted some pillows on her bed and grabbed all of them in one big swoop.

"Okay, guys. I can do the rest by myself."

Brennan ignored her grousing and placed three lavender pillows under her bare foot. He lingered his fingers on top of her still swollen and cold skin of her ankle. "You got peas in the freezer?"

"I'm on it," Calum said.

Brennan took her ballet slippers from his back pockets and laid them on the floor next to her bedside table. He perched his sizeable frame on the side of the bed, making the bed dip so she had to place her hand on his bicep to not fall over to his side. She groaned, his sudden move tweaking her ankle.

"Shit. This is some fucked-up bed you have here."

"There is nothing wrong with my bed, thank you very much. Perhaps my bed isn't made for a six foot four guy who weighs two hundred and thirty pounds. Maybe you should lie off the chicken wings from Lucky?"

He snorted. "Six foot five. And two hundred and fifty pounds."

He grinned when her eyes widened and roamed his muscular thighs, broad chest and iron pumped arms. He kept in shape, and she sure appreciated his physique—no doubt about it.

Errin cleared her throat and narrowed her eyes. "Well, my bed isn't used to a big ape sitting on it. So scram."

He guffawed at her bluntness, but she had another thing coming if she thought he'd let her dismiss him.

"Oh, what guys do you usual bring home then? Are you into the nerdy skinny type? Some guy that can't even ripple this miserable bed?"

"If I had a type, it wouldn't be an oversized, overbearing—"

She trailed off when Calum entered the room. He placed a mug on her bedside table and the sweet aroma of hot chocolate filled the air. Errin's scowl made room for a loving smile for her big brother.

Damn, but Brennan wanted to be on the receiving end of that sweet smile. *What the fuck?* He'd been so sleep deprived that he was losing his mind. He got up from the bed and her hand jutted out to catch herself again.

Calum placed a fluorescent popsicle against her ankle. She grimaced. The ice-cold popsicle was relentless and didn't mold to her skin.

"What the fuck is that?" Brennan asked.

Calum narrowed his eyes at Brennan. "What? Couldn't find frozen peas in the freezer. So this will have to do for now. You got a better idea?"

Errin shifted her foot on the pillow and scrunched her face up.

"You don't got any lying around in case shit like this happens?"

Errin waved a single hand in the air, dismissing the mere idea of having them. "I hate peas. Can't stand the icky structure. Yuck. But ice cream, Cal? Really? Just take the damn thing away."

"Ye don't have to eat the damn peas, just have the bag in the back of ye freezer," Calum mumbled under his breath as he stomped out of the room with the popsicle.

Brennan glanced at Errin. "Okay. I'm going to—"

"Yeah, thank you for taking me to the ER," Errin said. "And for taking me home, I guess. I'm sure my brother can take it from here."

He nodded and turned on his heels before he could do something stupid. Something like going through her freezer to find something that *would* work. Or rearranging those pillows under her ankle just to feel her soft skin again.

A firm hand grabbed his shoulder in the hallway, right before he opened the front door even further. Ah, big brother isn't done just yet. He and Calum mirrored each other not only in size, but also in the blunt way they went about things. He picked up on that shit when he first met Calum six months ago when he'd visited Errin's sister, Kayla, here in Austin.

"What's going on here?" Calum asked.

"I know... coming home at this hour and seeing she's hurt her ankle—"

"Fuck. What it is with you Mills brothers? One by one, my sisters all fall for you," Calum groused.

"Not a chance in hell!" Errin bellowed from her bedroom down the hall. *Shit, this apartment is made of paper.*

Brennan chuckled at Errin's feisty response, even though her quick rejection of them ever getting together bugged him. Calum smirked.

"Look. I appreciate you letting her crash at your place. When she'd texted me last night, I figured it was just that. Nothing more."

Brennan nodded in confirmation.

"So, there isn't more going on here?" Calum jutted his chin and waited for Brennan to answer him. He cocked his head, letting his almost white blonde hair fall over his raised eyebrow.

"You heard her, man. Not a chance in hell."

During his drive home, this weird feeling crept up on him. Something about her response nagged at him.

Last night and this morning had come out of left field and, of course, they wouldn't kiss ever again. Calum's drill for answers was the wake-up call he needed. They were close to family now that her sisters were romantically involved with his brothers. Time to nip whatever the fuck this was in the bud.

At the pub, he glanced at the clock above the bar and sure enough; he had two hours left to get some sleep. He left the cash register for now. Things would be slow, since it was the day after Halloween. Who in their right mind would go to Lucky at eleven in the morning?

He walked up the stairs to the apartment and the smell of fried bacon and eggs welcomed him. Pops hunched over the dingy stove whilst humming along with Sinatra's 'Fly me to the moon'.

"Ah, boyo! Come sit with yer old grandfather for a bit."

"I just got back from—"

"Yes, I just hung up the phone with Bunny. Glad our lass is gonna be all right." Pops glanced at Brennan over his shoulder.

"She's not mine, Pops."

"Sit." Pops clanked a plate full of toast, fried eggs, and bacon in front of him before turning around to crack another egg in the sizzling pan for himself.

The Sinatra song from last night filled the kitchen, and Pops sang along while flipping his omelet in the pan. "I tried so, not to give in... I said to myself this affair, it never will go so well..."

Brennan shook his head and smiled at his grandfather. Pops was on a roll now.

He knew better than to go against Pops when he was in this kind of mood. He was like a shark detecting a drop of blood in the water. Pops was free from doubt something was going on between him and Errin, and now he was circling and circling, ready to take a bite.

"Ever really listened to Frank, boyo? And think hard before you answer me. Did you ever *really* listen to the guy?"

"Can't say I have," Brennan said after he swallowed half of his toast in one bite. He stood and grabbed a jug of orange juice from the fridge. He took another glass from the creaking cabinet and poured them both a glass.

Pops placed his full plate on the kitchen table. They ate with Sinatra's crooning filling the silence, and Brennan wondered how long it'd take Pops to broach the subject of Errin.

But after polishing his plate clean, Pops took their plates to the tiny sink and washed them both. Brennan dried the dishes before placing them back in the cupboards.

As they stood side by side, doing the day-to-day chore of the dishes, the love and respect between them washed over him. Sudden emotions often overwhelmed him regarding his grandfather. Knowing what it was like to miss a loved one, he was grateful to have Pops still by his side.

His relationship with his father had been strained after his mother died. Pops had filled Sean Jr.'s spot as a father figure and he'd been everything Brennan wanted to grow up as. This strong and burly man who loved his family with all of his heart and fought for them no matter what was what first drew Brennan to Lucky.

The responsibility of running the pub had made his father absent while growing up, leaving Brennan the man of the house at age fourteen. He stepped up to take care of his four younger brothers whenever their dad was out at Lucky or sleeping in after a late night hanging out with the regulars at the bar.

It's solely for the love of Pops and his love for Lucky that Brennan long ago decided he'd eventually take his father's place. In a few weeks' time, Brennan will be the third generation Mills running the joint. He was more determined than ever to make Pops proud of him.

Pops slapped him on the back of his head and he dropped a plate on the kitchen counter with a loud clatter.

"Ye can't treat her like any other lass, ye hear? Errin—"

"Pops—"

Brennan wanted to reassure him he had no intentions at all with Errin, but Pops narrowed his eyes under his bushy gray brows. That look alone shut Brennan up.

"As I was sayin'... seein' ye holdin' Errin last night was somethin' special. Now, I love the Walsh girls with all of me heart. Hell, every one of those Walshes I consider family now. But me Bunny lass...."

Pops shook his head and smiled. He cleared his throat and dropped the smile from his face.

"Right. Just be one hundred percent sure before ye act, is all I say. Don't want to miss her pretty little face and big mouth, ye hear. And don't make me go after yer arse for ever hurtin' her."

With a nod of his head, Brennan said, "Understood."

Austin

Errin
5

"Thanks again for taking us home, Cait," Calum said. He opened the door to Errin and Cait's apartment building, and Cait motioned for Errin to hop through first while Calum held the door for her. Errin's other brother Conner pushed the elevator button.

"No problem at all, you guys," Cait said.

Errin looked up at Caitlin, AKA the brunette bombshell living next door to Errin. When her sister Kayla first had moved into Errin's apartment, Cait and Kayla became instant best friends.

Errin would often tag along on their girls' night out. Cait was outgoing, always spoke her mind, and as a cop, Cait wasn't a dainty girl's girl, which Errin appreciated.

"I can't believe Kayla won game night *again*. Even partnered up with Dunc, she wins," Cait said.

Errin grinned.

"I still can't believe you didn't get me on 'shoveling snow'." Calum chuckled.

"I'm a Texas girl. I figured you were pitching horseshit with a fork. Not snow."

Everyone laughed.

"What? I can count the times I've seen snow on both hands." Cait shrugged.

"Yeah, okay. We're used to it over in Jersey," Conner said.

Her brother Calum pushed the button for the elevator again.

Errin figured he was eager to finally stay over at Cait's tonight. They'd danced around each other for several months now, and tonight had been the first time Cait invited him over at her place. Calum's crush on Cait was getting legendary in the Walsh family.

When they got on the elevator, Cait blushed. Calum ground his teeth and was about to combust, as he focused his eyes on Cait.

"What did one plate whisper to the other plate?" Errin asked, balancing on her crutches.

Calum groaned in annoyance, but Caitlin grinned.

Conner leaned in and said in a low, fake voice, "Are you also hot, plate?"

They all laughed, but Errin shook her head. She glanced at Calum and he said, "Want to lick me clean?"

"Eww, that's disgusting Cal!" Errin shouted.

Calum winked at Cait and she bumped her hip into his while laughing along with the rest of them.

"Cait?"

"Uhm, I have no idea. Er..." she shot a look at Calum, but he wasn't helping at all as he gave her a lopsided grin, getting her even more flustered.

Errin revealed the answer before they would arrive at their floor. "Dinner is on me."

She laughed the loudest at her own joke, which happened a lot. The doors of the elevator opened, and they stepped into the hallway. Errin hopped on her crutches in front of the others and as she placed her key in the door, she said goodnight to Calum and Cait.

A muffled reply escaped Cait. Errin glanced over her

shoulder to see that her brother had Cait backed up to the door to her apartment and was pretty well chewing her face off.

"Why is 'drool' the most favorite word of all time?" Conner boomed across the hallway.

Errin poked him in the side, but he shrugged her off.

"Because it just rolls off the tongue."

When no one responded, Errin opened the door and entered her narrow hallway. She shook her head at Conner, who still was laughing behind her. He took his coat off to hang on the rack.

"He's a goner. As soon as Kate moves in with Donovan, you've got yourself a new roommate." He snickered.

What? Kate's moving out? Calum moving in? Oh, hell no! Errin swirled around in her sensible sneakers, forgetting to keep her balance on her crutches, and cried out in pain.

"Fuck. Come here, Bunny." Conner picked her up in his sturdy arms, grabbing both crutches in one hand. He walked them over to the pink worn sofa and let her crutches crash to the floor. They sat down on the couch and he handed her the gray fleece blanket from the back of the couch.

"Okay. Time to spill it. What the fuck is going on here?" He used his serious big brother tone.

"There is nothing—" she pulled the blanket over her outstretched legs.

"Hmm-mm. Right," Conner drawled.

"Nothing to spill, really. I was drunk off my ass last night. You know I can't drink like the rest of you. Those tequila shots floored me. As I've texted you and every other overbearing Walsh brother—"

"Whatever," he said, rolling his eyes at his sister.

"That I would spend the night over at Brennan's. So I woke up in the middle of the night, got up from his bed and—"

"Wait a minute." Conner held up his hand to interrupt. "You slept with him?"

"No, I didn't sleep with Broody Brennan!" she all but shouted at her brother.

"Broody Brennan?" he snorted with his brows pulled together.

"Yeah, well... he's kinda mysterious and.... Stop looking at me like that." She ducked her head and rubbed an imaginary piece of dust from her blanket.

"What? You've never—*ever* described a guy being 'mysterious' before." He smirked and tilted his head.

"Well, that ain't right. I've been with a lot of mysterious guys before." She looked him straight into his light blue eyes. The exact same color she saw everyday staring back at her in the mirror while doing her make-up.

They had the same eyes. Same wavy, warm blonde hair. People guessed they were twins, even though they were several years apart.

"Nah, you can try to irritate me but I'm sticking on this subject, Bunny. Now, tell me what happened. Why are you so secretive? Just spill the beans. It isn't like you to hold your tongue—about anything."

"We kissed, okay? Happy now?" she pouted and crossed her arms in front of her chest. She grimaced at the stinging pain in her ankle.

Conner went to the kitchen and rummaged around in her freezer. He pulled out one of the pea bags that Brennan had dropped off this morning. Brennan had mumbled something to Calum about having too many bags of peas at the pub, and he figured he'd give some to her for her ankle. And he was right. The swelling had gone down before game night at Kayla and Duncan's. But standing and walking back and forth from the car hadn't been the best of ideas.

Conner rested her ankle on top of two throw pillows on the coffee table and took off her sneaker and sock. He sat down next to her foot and held the frozen pea bag on the damned ankle.

"Do you want to talk for real now or do you want to hear another stupid joke?" He rearranged the frozen bag over her ankle. He evaded her eyes. Everyone knew it was hard for Errin to talk about her feelings.

Errin had no problem talking someone's ears off about anything and everything. Even when she met a person for the first time, she often ended up having the weirdest conversations about aliens or online life hack videos showing how to easily peel garlic or remove the skin from roasted peanuts.

She often talked with Maureen, her seventy-six-year-old neighbor, about old movies, Coco Chanel, and other vintage stuff. She trash talked with her brothers and now even with the Mills brothers here in Austin. Errin always spoke her mind. Without a doubt, she rubbed people the wrong way with her confrontational questions or crude remarks.

But talking about her feelings? No. That's not Errin. She never let people close enough to see inside her head.

She had opened up to Pops last night and laid all her cards on the table. She'd confided in him about how unhappy and sometimes even miserable she's been in Austin. She'd been rejected yet again for an audition, and now she'd taken on this literally shitty job at the dog kennel.

She loved nothing more than dancing, but that wasn't working out. The last time she'd danced professionally had been months ago, back in Jersey.

Her sisters were solely focused on their boyfriends and had started an actual life out here in Austin with proper jobs and new friends. Although she lived with Kate, her sister only ever came home to pack a fresh change of clothes to take with her back to Donovan's.

Errin's homesick phone calls over the last few weeks to her brother Conner and the rest of her family back home were getting longer and more frequent. But now there was this broody, attentive, and gorgeous guy who interfered with her pity party.

"I don't know, Con. I..." she shook her head.

Conner sighed but didn't push it.

"He gets under my skin," she said. "You know? He's just this old moody guy, always grumpy and ready to speak his mind and give people his two cents."

"Are you talking about Pops or Brennan here?" Conner grinned.

"Brennan, of course," Errin snapped.

"Well, sorry to burst your bubble. I know how much you've grown to love the old man, but you just described Brennan exactly like Pops."

Errin busted out laughing, not taking his words seriously. She clutched her side.

"No, for real. Listen," he said, holding up his fingers to tick off each item. "Old. Grumpy. And always speaking his mind."

She shook her head in denial. Could it be? Did she like Brennan? Okay, the man is hot as sin. But now she even *liked* him? Like *really* liked him?

"Why did you lie to Kate about hurting your ankle while stretching?"

Her brother knew there had to be a reason for Errin to keep a secret from her sister. The Walsh sisters told each other everything. But she didn't want to get into it now. What was she to say? Kate was never around anymore and when she was, she wasn't involved.

Earlier, Errin tried to downplay what happened at Brennan's. Her sister Kate had asked her about her ankle during game night in front of everyone. Luckily, the one Mills brother who'd been absent tonight was Brennan.

"Con, I love Kate. I really do. But lately, we're just not that close. She's always spending the night over at Donovan's or having lunch with Bree, her new BFF."

"Well, how do you think I feel with thousands of miles between me and my sisters? Do you think your brothers don't miss you girls?"

"Yeah, I know, but—"

Conner shook his head. "No, Bunny. Think about it."

He motioned his hand in between them. "We make it work. We text, right?"

Errin nodded and released a big breath.

"I see your big mouth almost every other day via a video call. I see more of you now than when you were living just a train ride away." He chuckled, and she joined him after playfully slapping his chest.

"So. What you mean is that I have to video call Kate?"

"No. Well, not exactly. What I mean to say is that you have to make it work. Kate isn't the only one responsible here. You can get your butt off the couch and see her too, you know?"

"Yeah, yeah. I hear you," Errin mumbled.

"Hmm-hmm."

"I said I hear you. Now, can you please help me to my bedroom?"

Errin had enough talking about her sister. She loved Kate. But living in the same city, hell—sharing an apartment together, but still feeling thousands of miles apart was not something she'd liked to talk about. Not even with her brother and best friend.

After showering and hopping over to her bed, she took the purple comforter in hand to pull it open. She thought of Brennan doing the same earlier today.

After bringing her to the ER and waiting for hours in the hospital in the waiting room with her, Brennan had taken the time to make sure she was being looked after at home. He brought those gross bags of peas even though he'd been scheduled to work at Lucky this morning.

He had even texted her tonight to see how she was holding up. He didn't respond to the last text she'd send him, but it was sweet of him to check up on her.

She nestled in her bed, picked up her phone and opened the Lucky profile on social media. She clicked on a picture of Brennan and Emmy, Lucky's cook and Brennan's cousin. He smiled at his cousin in the photo, and it made Errin's heart flutter.

Errin wasn't the only woman stalking the handsome bartender online. Pff. Some seriously desperate Seeking Susan's commented with drooling emoji's and wide eyes smileys. Not that he'd ever reply.

She'd done her research. He may not be a choirboy, but out of all the Mills brothers, Brennan and Declan were the two most reserved. They didn't seem to sleep around that much. Well, not like their brother, Ronan, the manwhore.

She smiled and shook her head as she typed a comment under one photo. It was a cute picture of Brennan's dad bringing in her birthday cake into the pub yesterday. She typed and hit send.

Let's see if he'll reply.

Brennan woke up to a notification from his phone. He turned on his side, making his old bed groan, and grabbed the annoying fucker from his nightstand. Brennan had recently decided to close Lucky on Mondays, and he would've slept in today if it weren't for this unknown number, texting him at nine in the morning.

He skimmed the text. Janessa. Some barfly at the pub. How she ended up with his number, he had no clue. He deleted her text without replying and blocked her number.

He'd told her months ago he wasn't interested. Her keeping up her stalking ways proved his instincts were right once again. Growing up around the bar gave him a sixth sense in reading people.

He scrolled through his texts and came across Errin's juvenile response from yesterday. He'd texted her to ask how she was doing after he'd handed over the frozen pea bags to her brother. And surprise, surprise... When she'd finally replied, she'd already been walking around, going over to Duncan's house for monthly game night. Right after she'd been told to rest her ankle for about a week.

Now how was that helping? To say it irritated him would be an understatement. If he hadn't scared Errin, she'd never have fallen and sprained her ankle. So he wanted to make sure she would be all right. But did she care?

No.

After he'd texted her late last night to point out she was sabotaging her recovery, she'd sent a meme to him of a woman standing in a backyard on a ladder, peering through a binocular with the following text underneath: Me looking for a fuck to give... Can't find one tho.

After that entertaining response, he wasn't reaching out to her anymore. If she wanted to fuck up her recovery and act like a petulant child, he'd no longer care. So he didn't reply to her meme and went to sleep. Still lying in bed with his phone in hand, he blinked when Declan's name filled the screen.

"What's up?" Brennan said after clearing his throat.

"Bren, shit, man. I forgot it's Monday. Did I wake you?"

"No, no. Was already up."

"Okay. Good," Declan said. He remained silent.

"What's going on?" Brennan asked. His brother often turned to Brennan for advice, and he guessed the reason for Dec's phone call had something to do with Bree.

"Squirt." Declan sighed.

Ding, ding, ding. Bree hated the nickname the Mills brothers gave her when she was six and had just moved in next door with her parents and four sisters. But the name suited her, as she was the little squirt following the Mills boys around from the tree house on whatever adventure.

Bree was two years younger than Declan, but the two were so close growing up, people often thought she was part of the Mills family instead of a Ryan girl. Things weren't so good at home for a while after Bree's father left when Bree was nine. She would stay over at the Mills place more often than not.

"Tell me," Brennan said.

"I know I should forget her. Ronan said—"

"Stop listening to your damn twin, Dec." Brennan shifted to sit up in his bed and furrowed his brows at the mention of Ronan, telling his brother to forget Bree.

"He's an idiot. You realize why he's so adamant to keep you and Bree apart? He's still not over her sister, and my guess is he never will. If he didn't mess things up with Fianna, he would root for you and Bree the loudest."

Brennan remained silent for a few beats. Declan mulled over his words, often needing to use his oldest brother as a sounding board. Sure, the twins shared a unique bond no one could ever come between, but they were polar opposites.

Declan, the first-born twin by mere minutes, was a dutiful cop who always thought things through before acting. The exact opposite of Ronan. He was loud, often obnoxious, rough around the edges, but had a big heart. As an MMA fighter, Ronan doesn't want people to see him as some overgrown teddy bear. But his close family got his number a long time ago.

"She's still seeing that nerd from work. Went out with him last night."

Brennan rolled his eyes.

"Ye broke her heart when ye told her ye didn't love her like she loved ye. What did'ya think was gonna happen, Dec?"

Grumbles traveled the line, but Declan didn't answer his rhetoric question. So Brennan pushed further in his agitated Irish brogue.

"A beautiful girl like Bree—who's followed ye around like a lovesick puppy... since the moment ye first laid eyes on her, who's been waiting on ye stupid arse for years... And now, now she's *finally* moving on, ye come whining she's dating some nerd? Why do ye care?"

"I... shit..." he said, followed by another sigh.

"Dec. You need to tell her how you feel, man."

"Yeah. Cait's been saying the same thing."

Partnered up with Bree's sister Cait on the police force, Declan was close with not one, but two Ryan sisters. And more often than not, Cait gave Dec her two cents about him messing things up with her younger sister.

"Unless ye don't love her? If she's not the one, leave her the fuck alone. Understood? Squirt deserves a man who fights for her. So if ye really love her—and we all know ye do—go after her, bro." Brennan grabbed a glass of water from his nightstand and took a few gulps.

"Thanks Bren. I guess I needed to hear that. Some things have happened between us, but I was thinking it wasn't fair to come at her with this shit now she's seeing that chump. But you're right. I'm gonna go after what I want—what I need."

"Thank fuck for that," Brennan said before he downed the last of the water.

"I'll talk to you later," Declan said.

"Yeah. Let me know what she says, man."

"Will do," Dec said as his voice trailed off.

"And Dec?"

"Yeah?"

"I'm proud of ye," Brennan said before hanging up, not waiting for Dec's response. The Mills men didn't do mushy girl talk. But he was proud of Dec and wasn't ashamed to tell him.

He turned to his other side and opened his social media sites one by one and scrolled through last night's reactions.

Their family's pub needed to be more visible online, and he was the lucky loser with that shitty job. He hated the whole nine yards about these sites with their fake, cheery people who pretended to live the perfect life.

<3_Errin_Bunny_<3 also commented on Lucky Irishman's post: "Best birthday party ever! Thxxx"

<3_Errin_Bunny_<3 liked your photo

There she was again.

He'd posted a picture of a very packed pub during the annual Halloween party, but that had been two nights ago, right after his father had entered with Errin's birthday cake and she'd reunited with her brothers.

He tapped the heart button on his screen—next to her comment, coloring the heart shape dark pink. Before he could back out, he looked her up from his private account to shoot a DM to her.

BRENNAN: Of course it was the best you've ever had.

Okay. He was officially losing his mind. He was now even messaging the girl? And fuck if she didn't respond immediately.

ERRIN: Cocky much?

He hoisted himself up the bed into a sitting position, with his back against the wall, and crossed his feet with his long outstretched legs before typing his reply.

BRENNAN: You've seen nothing yet...

She was typing, and he smiled, thinking she surely would sass him after his not-so-subtle innuendo.

ERRIN: If you're about to send me a dick pic... don't bother.

He laughed and plotted a sharp response, but another message already popped up.

ERRIN: Now if you'd send me a pic of your hairy chest instead... I'm totally here for that.

Hairy chest? What was that supposed to mean? He kept his chest hair neat, no overgrown hairy jungle for him. She already sent another message, giving him no time to respond.

ERRIN: You can pick any part of me... what would you like to see?

Fuck. Fuck. Fuck. It's Errin he's messaging here, not some random chick from the pub. He was playing with fire, but what was he to do now? Stop and not respond? Well, that would be just rude. Not to mention a dick move.

Okay. Think. Nothing overly sexy, to direct their exchange into PG waters, so to speak. When thinking of Errin, what would he picture? Hmm, right. Should he send his request? She would hate his answer and wouldn't go for it. No doubt. *Ah, fuck it.*

BRENNAN: Your smile.

He kept on typing, but she also typed. He hit send to beat her to the punch, because he wanted to give more explanation about the reason he wanted her smile, out of everything he could have picked.

BRENNAN: But I don't want the smile you give to everyone.

She typed and typed, like she had deleted her original answer and started her reply all over again.

ERRIN: Oh, so now I even have special kinds of smiles? Quite the revelation.

He was about to reveal way too much here, but he wasn't backing down now.

BRENNAN: You have a smile for every fuckin' stranger at the pub. The smile that says you're in for a friendly conversation.

He kept on typing.

BRENNAN: You have a special smile for your family. If they're around, your eyes light up like Christmas lights.

He hit send and kept typing.

BRENNAN: But whenever you and Pops are together, your smile is contagious. It even makes me smile.

Okay, there was no stopping this now...

BRENNAN: But the smile I want from you... is the smile you haven't given to anyone else before.

He doubted she would send him something at all, but as if on cue, a picture popped up on his screen. Would she play along or try to skirt around his sudden but obvious interest in her bubbly persona? He hadn't even realized he'd observed her like this in these past months.

Asking for a picture of her tits or arse was in Errin's case much more of a safe bet, being more impersonal than what he'd asked of her now. He'd seen enough of Errin in the brief time she'd lived in Austin to know one thing for certain: she didn't let anyone get close to her. Well, except her family. And possibly his grandfather.

He tapped the picture to enlarge. *Hmm, figures.* Such an Errin move to send him a picture of her perky tits instead. Anything to maintain a certain emotional distance between them. Now, there's definitely nothing wrong with these smaller, but still beautiful round globes, pushing against the dark purple lace. It was like they were just begging for him to suck, nibble and bite them.

His dick twitched, and he grabbed a hold of it through his black boxer briefs, feeling his length hardening beneath his fingers. Under her tits, he spotted a toned waist and was that a belly button piercing? A tattoo over her left ribs drew his attention, but he couldn't make out the words in this angle.

ERRIN: Cat got your tongue?

She had the audacity to ask. He needed to reply, but he'd been too busy leering at her tits.

BRENNAN: Fuck. Can't even think of anything smart to type. All my blood went from my brain to my dick...

She sent a blushing emoji,

ERRIN: So, think you can return the favor?

Okay. A picture of his chest would be no problem. He just had to make sure his now raging hard-on was out of the picture. But first he needed to reply.

BRENNAN: Your picture wasn't exactly what I asked for, Lips. Not that I'm complaining... Followed by a drooling emoji.

He hit send and kept typing.

BRENNAN: But next time I see you, you better give me that smile...

He opened the camera app and flexed his muscles for the picture. Shit, he needed to get it from another angle and stood from his bed. He walked into his attached bathroom and switched the lights on.

He shook his head at his reflection in the bathroom mirror: a thirty-seven-year-old man, squinting at his own reflection, deepening the crowfeet next to his light green eyes, rubbing the three days' worth of stubble on his chiseled chin.

He was about to send the youngest sister of his brother's girlfriends, a picture of him—half naked. He'd sent a picture like this before, but that had been to his girlfriend at the time.

Errin replied before he could take a picture, making him groan out loud as he read it.

ERRIN: How about this... next time I see you, I'll be wearing my biggest, brightest smile and nothing else?

She was killing him here. Now he pictured her taunting him, as she stood naked before him. He took out his dick from his boxers and stroked it from base to tip. After a few hard strokes, the telltale tingles surfaced and traveled his spine. How in the hell did she get him so worked up already?

Another notification pinged on his phone, and he grabbed it from the counter.

ERRIN: Are you still there? Or are your hands otherwise engaged?

Mmm, always that fuckin' sass on her. What he wouldn't do for a chance to put her hands and lips into a better use right now. He pictured her plump, pink lips enveloping his thick base, giving his dick a warm welcome into her luscious mouth.

She would lick him while fisting his cock with her small hand. Repeatedly licking and sucking him further in. He would tower over her, as she would connect those sweet aquamarine orbs with his green eyes.

Oh, his hand would go from her cheek up into her hairline, where his fingers would glide through her gorgeous warm blonde strands, as she would swallow around him.

He pumped faster and faster, making his toes curl and his muscles flex while he groaned out his release. "Fuuuck." After catching his breath, he turned on the faucet and washed away his cum from the bathroom sink.

He opened the shower stall and turned on the spray before he ridded himself from his boxer briefs. After stepping under the scalding water, a vision of Errin popped up in his mind. The petite vixen who needed to stay in control by sending him a picture of her tits, instead of a simple photo of her smile. Complicated and puzzling, all wrapped up in fuckin' sexy purple lace.

Never mind coming just moments ago, his dick already hardened while picturing Errin in that erotic piece of fabric. Shit, he still hadn't replied to her. Now that wasn't very gentlemanlike of him. He would have to rectify this situation immediately. He opened the shower stall and grabbed his phone from the counter.

He covered his chest with a handful of shower gel and let the sandalwood-scented suds trail down to his abs. He shot the pictures while holding his phone just outside the shower door.

After taking and scrutinizing another three pictures, he sent the best one to Errin. It showed his erect nipples and his shiny, wet chest hair, sticking to his tanned skin above his six-pack, with a little start of the V shape going further down.

He turned the showerhead toward the tiles in the stall's corner to stand partially under the spray without getting his phone wet. By placing the device on the integrated shampoo ledge at eye level, he monitored their rendezvous if she'd reply him.

She received his picture and one quick response after the other came in.

ERRIN: Fuck. That's hot.

ERRIN: I was wondering what took you so long.

ERRIN: The thought of you naked in the shower right now... mmm.

ERRIN: Not coming without me, I hope?

He grinned because he already came so hard. It had been a long time since he came with such force by his own hand. But he could still easily go for another round.

He made good use of the shower gel as he soaped his upper body once more, trailing his soapy hand down to his dick. He took another picture with his other hand, as he aimed to send something to make her squirm even more.

The next picture he took was of him engulfing his cock with soapy suds while grabbing a hold of it. Okay. That wasn't bad at all. He didn't want to scare Errin off by sending his long and thick equipment in full glory. But this picture with his hand and the suds partially surrounding his dick would do the trick. *Right. Send.*

ERRIN: Oh... my...

And then... nothing. He endured several minutes with no further response while he kept glancing at his phone that stood on the shampoo ledge again, leaning against the wall.

Was she shocked that he sent a dick pic to her? Or was she... the image of Errin masturbating entered his mind. Was she circling her clit over and over with her fingers? Or did she have a favorite toy she'd use?

BRENNAN: I want to hear you come.

He typed hastily and clicked the send button. With one hand, he squeezed beneath the crown of his dick to keep from coming again and with his other hand; he called her to phone her hands free. Well, not exactly hands free since he still held his dick in his hand.

He turned down the water spray to an absolute minimum so he wouldn't get too cold and moved closer to his phone on the ledge. In this position, he could talk and jerk off while the hot water spray still caressed his back. She needed to pick up the phone real quick or else he would blow without her.

She picked up after the third dial tone. She didn't say a word; the only sound that traveled the line was her heavy breathing. The sweetest soft little moan escaped her.

"Fuck baby, you're playing with yourself?" he asked as he pumped his dick again.

"Hmm-mm, I... I..." she spoke so softly, like she was afraid to be overheard or something.

"You alone?" he demanded.

"Yesss..." she breathed.

He rested his forehead against the wet tiles and moaned as goose bumps traveled over his back.

"Ooh, the way you moan in my ear, Bren. Ooooh... I... can't."

"I wish I could see you right now. Are you in bed?"

"Yes," she whispered.

"Are you still wearing that fuckin' purple bra?" he threw out.

"Hmm-mm."

"I'm almost there. I need to hear ye. Tell me what you're doing," he said.

She moaned, "I can't... I'm going to... Bren!"

"Aaah." He let out all his pent up frustration from delaying his second orgasm. But fuck, it had been worth the wait. Errin was in total ecstasy, so hot and unabashed about fucking herself with Brennan listening in on her.

She heaved a sigh in satisfaction and he felt like he won the jackpot. Okay, he may not have laid a single finger on her, but she'd screamed out *his* name as she came.

He altered the spray's direction and washed away his cum from the shower tiles. She giggled in his ear and his upper lip tugged up at her sweet sound. Now she even had him smiling. What was this little spitfire doing to him?

"So, I guess now isn't the right time to tell a joke, but I just don't do awkward after sex, so listen up."

He shook his head, smiling, but didn't speak up.

"So I tried phone sex once... but the phone was kinda big and I hurt my ass," Errin said and he heard her smile.

He bellowed a laugh but didn't hear her response. It was like the line went dead. He eyed his phone, expecting a black screen with the dead battery sign—but he still had seventy-three percent remaining.

Did she just hang up on his arse? *'I just don't do awkward after sex?'* What the fuck was up with that?

Errin

7

"How nice of you to finally grace us with your presence. What was it this time? Let me guess, you had a gas leak at home?" Casey sneered from somewhere behind the reception desk.

Only her pitch-black strands, cut in a short bob, showed as she sat on her chair and leaned to the side, probably to pet some stray lice ball.

"Oh, no, wait. Don't tell me. Your car broke down? Or the bus took a wrong turn?" Casey pulled herself up and leered over the thick, dark-rimmed glasses resting on the tip of her nose.

A week ago, after taking the picture of the kennel, Errin promptly found herself in a job interview with the owner, Colleen. They'd hit it off, and although Errin hated dogs with a passion, she desperately needed a job. Since she didn't get the part in this musical out in Jersey, she now had to deal with these stinking, barking, biting and shitting mongrels.

And let's not forget Colleen's daughter and co-owner, Casey. Her snarky attitude had more bite to it now that Errin had a mere four hours of sleep last night before she dragged her ass over to work.

The goodbyes to her brothers at the airport had been very emotional for all the Walsh siblings. The moment she had gotten used to having her brothers back around, they went back home to Jersey.

Errin swallowed back a response and decided just this once —and for this time only—she would ignore Casey's snotty remarks.

No, she would not stoop to her level today. She would let things slide and take the high road just for once in her life. Come on, did she always had to speak up when someone would bitch to her? Nah. Forget about Casey. She had to be *the very last person* on the list to waste her time and energy on.

She limped around the reception desk and Casey talked in her signature high-pitched pet voice. Like she was talking to a baby, but she yapped to a wide-eyed Chihuahua rescue dog, shuddering on her lap. "Now, Chico, did you see her ignoring mommy? Bad, bad Errin. Yes, my little prince," she said, holding the dog in her stick figure arms.

"Did you hear about the Chihuahua that killed the German Shepard?" Errin asked.

Casey startled. "Um, no. Why? What happened?" she furrowed her brows.

"It got stuck in his throat." Errin shook with laughter after Casey pursed her lips and turned her head away from Errin.

Errin had figured out a long time ago that she wasn't everybody's cup of tea. She could be a bit too much, always speaking her mind and laughing the loudest.

While growing up, she often experienced that not everyone handled her energy. Her family didn't call her Bunny after the Energizer Bunny for nothing.

But being loud didn't mean she loved to steal someone's limelight by putting others down or putting herself first. She loved to spend time with people, to have deep conversations and listen to their stories. But when someone was a total bitch to her? Well, she wasn't like her sister Kate.

Errin would *always* fight back. And by doing so, she often made matters worse. *But fuck it. And most of all—fuck Casey*.

She was right on time this morning, so where did Casey come off talking to her like that? Okay, she had been late a few times in the week she'd worked here. But it wasn't like she would also leave right on the dot every day.

That damned ankle was already weighing her down. She'd brought one crutch with her on the bus to walk around—albeit slow. She'd put some sports tape on her injury, just in case the swelling returned. She balanced on the one crutch and peered at Casey, but Casey didn't give her the time of day.

She didn't even mention anything about the damn crutch or even ask her if she was doing okay. Ugh, nevermind. Errin needed to get going if she was to walk all the dogs in the morning and throw some balls around in the park to give the mutts some exercise.

She entered the room with the sixteen crates, filled with rescue dogs in all shapes and sizes. Jacky was barking his ugly little head off. On the first day, the Jack Russell Terrier had gone straight for her calf with his sharp teeth when she opened his door. She wasn't making that mistake again, not while being this wobbly on her feet.

Normally she would take three or four social dogs at a time to the park and take the assholes alone out. But she couldn't make the normal six runs to the park with this ankle. The assholes, as she'd called the anti-social dogs, just had to play nice and tag along with the rest.

She'd have to take eight dogs at a time to reduce the number of runs to two. No biggie. Just be the alpha of the pack, right?

She took a deep breath, straightened her shoulders and hopped on one crutch to the back of the kennel. She would take Jacky out of his jail cell last and make him fall in line with the rest of the fuckers. *Yeah, keep on dreaming.*

She'd put the leashes on the first eight dogs and walked them out of the kennel, leaving her crutch behind. It was kind of a hassle, but so far so good.

The November morning air chilled her face. Nothing like she was used to back home, but still. She wore scuffed sneakers, dirty faded boyfriend jeans with a dark blue cable sweater that had gathered enormous holes. She would definitely not waste any quality stuff from her closet at the Pawty Hard Kennel.

The struggle of keeping the hairy bunch in line was keeping her warm, but Jacky was pulling like he was in for a race. She jerked his leash.

"Jacky, no. Stay with us. Stop pulling," she said while grabbing a better hold of three other leashes in her right hand. One leash slipped through her fingers and Border Collie Jones ran around the corner like his ass was on fire.

"Jones!" she shouted, making the other dogs bark in angst.

"Fuck. Fuck. Fuck!"

She stomped in the direction Jones ran off to, but came to a standstill for an excruciating pain in her already hurt ankle. *Oh nooo.* That didn't feel right. Shit.

She needed to take better care of her injury. If she never got to dance again because of these damned dogs, she would regret it forever.

The dogs were barking and jerking their leashes. Jacky took the momentum and came after her with a nasty snarl while she tried to dodge his attack. His tiny but sharp teeth grabbed a hold of her jeans, but he missed her calf this time. He hung onto the underside of her jeans as she shook her leg to kick him off.

Another leash slipped and Missy ran off. The Doberman hightailed it out of there and nothing could stop her. During the altercation, Errin had walked a block and lost sight of the park.

With no visual on Missy and Jones, she had no clue if they were in the park. Argh, she needed to repatriate those deserters.

The dogs didn't belong to anyone at the moment, but still. She was responsible for their well-being and letting them run around the city wasn't in their best interest. She may not be a dog lover, but she had a heart.

"Joh-hones... Mihs-syyy... Come heeere."

Of course there was no trace of either dog in the park. She had six dogs left out of eight. That had to be a bad score. After searching them for over thirty minutes in all corners and under all benches in the park, she called in reinforcements.

"Hey! What's up?" Kayla said.

"Sis, I need your help," Errin said, holding the phone between her ear and shoulder. Two of the dogs jerked the leash again, and she dropped her phone.

"Ah. For crying out loud! Just leave me the fuck alone!" Errin screamed.

"Errin! Errin, what's going on?" Kayla's shouts reached her from the ground, just before big Al took the phone in his mouth and crunched it.

"No, no, nooo! Bad Al!" she said as she tried to save whatever left of her phone. The enormous Newfoundland dog sat on his ass and cocked his head, not having the slightest clue of what he'd done wrong.

She slumped onto the cold wooden seat of the bench closest to the park entrance and checked her phone. Nothing. Just a black, cracked screen.

"Okay. This ain't over 'till the fat lady sings."

One by one, she tied the dogs to the bench.

After another fifteen minutes, she spotted Missy sniffing behind a bush. She monitored the other dogs by the bench over her shoulder, but she couldn't risk it.

"Missy, come here. I've got a little treat for you..." she sing-songed.

Thank God that did the trick. The moment Missy was in

reach, Errin grabbed her leash and hopped over to the bench with the other six dogs tied to it. She had to sit down again, since the walk to catch Missy had been too much for her ankle.

She eyeballed Al, who gnawed on her phone, his newfound chew toy.

"Great. That's just reeeal great, Al. I hope you choke on it," she said as she eyed Al.

"You talking to dogs now?" a low voice said behind her.

She startled and whirled around in her seat.

Brennan smirked at her, hands gripping on the backrest. He wore a black sweater and dark blue jeans and looked good enough to eat, hair still wet from the shower. She blinked away the vision of a showering Brennan.

"You're going cuckoo on me?" he said as he cocked his head and raised a brow.

Errin shook her head to let his words register. "What?"

"Cuckoo. You know, bat shit crazy. Bonkers. Are you turning in some kind of lunatic, expecting for Al," he gestured at the dog laying at her feet still chewing on her phone, "To reply to you? Even with his mouth full, I might add?"

She snorted, annoyed with him. Why was he here? He wasn't supposed to run into her for quite some time, she'd decided yesterday. She wanted to steer clear of him, to let the memory of their phone sex episode fade away to the background. That way, she wouldn't be so tempted to jump his boner.

Geez, bones! Not boner. She had a one-track mind, ever since she'd screamed out his name in ecstasy. That beautiful, thick, long cock of his, surrounded by suds. Mmm. Oh, and what really rocked her boat? His moans as he was busy pleasuring himself.

She cleared her throat and scooted over to make room for his sizeable frame. He took a seat next to her and petted Missy.

The dog let him rub her behind her ears. Hmm, just another thing that ticked her off.

"What are you doing here?" She awkwardly petted Betty, a mixed-breed mutt. Brennan must've recognized in her movements she'd never pet a single dog in her entire life before, as he quirked a brow in question.

"Donovan called me and said Kayla called him in panic. She was worried something bad happened to you. You'd called and screamed for someone to leave you the fuck alone."

"Oh shit. Shit! I was talking to these damn dogs!" she said as she turned to him and held out her hand. "Can I use your phone? Need to call her back."

He shook his head, his damp hair swishing over his forehead. "Already called her the moment I saw you from a distance, talking to the dogs. She knows you're okay. I told her you'd call her later."

"Hmm. And Kayla just agreed?"

"Well, she might have said something about she'd better hear from you sooner than later." He smirked at the exact moment Errin snorted, recognizing Kayla's fiery response.

"When she tried to call you back, and you didn't answer, she called that hacker brother of mine to track you. He called the kennel because your phone still worked when you were there earlier. They said you always go to this park and because Lucky is only two blocks from here, I immediately ran out the door after Donovan called me."

"I'm so sorry. You must—"

"No need to be sorry, Errin. I'm just relieved you're okay. I saw you across the park and figured you were just walking your dogs."

She scoffed. "These assholes are not mine!"

Brennan laughed and shook his head. "You're the worst dog walker in the existence of dog walking."

"Ah, shut up. I really needed a job, so sue me. I just don't like dogs, okay? I'm more of a cat person. These big fuckers scare me half to death most of the time. And have you met sweet 'ole Jacky?" She waved at the miniature dog that already stood attention, ready to charge Brennan.

"No, can't say I've had the pleasure before."

"Well, let me tell you, it's no pleasure at all to meet this flesh tearing little monster. This piranha on paws is the scariest out of them all."

She narrowed her eyes at the dog and as if Jacky realized they were talking about him, he barked a couple times before going back to snarling.

"Okay. I get that. So... why did you call Kayla?" he asked.

Errin sighed before she locked eyes with him. "I lost a dog and—"

"You lost a dog?" he said as he quirked a brow and sat back with his back against the backrest.

"Yes. Well, two actually."

He bellowed a laugh, and the sudden sound made Jacky jump up. Errin scooted closer to Brennan, but before the dog even reached Errin, Brennan had already grabbed his leash and jerked him into a sitting position.

"Stay."

And surprisingly enough, Jacky stayed. The dog still eyed them both, but he didn't dare to move another muscle.

Brennan's manly sandalwood scent soothed her, and she didn't scoot back over.

"So you were talking to the dogs then? When you called Kayla?"

"Yes. I just found Missy and left out here somewhere is Jones. He's a Border Collie. You know the type? Lots of hair. Runs like he's on speed or something," she said, glancing up at him.

Brennan was a lot taller than her, and his robust physique

would come in handy right now. She figured that maybe his coming over to 'rescue her' wasn't so bad, since he could help her walk what's remaining of the pack back to the kennel.

He tapped her leg. "Do you think you can walk back by yourself? Or do you need me to carry you to the kennel?"

"Please? Sorry. I think it's better for my ankle if you'd carry me," she said while glancing up at him, smiling shyly.

"Fuckin' cute."

"What?" She cocked her head to the side and blinked up at him.

He took her face between his palms and trailed his thumbs over her dimpled cheeks, making her eyes flutter closed. While leaning down to her, his mint breath tickled her face as he whispered, "Your... blush."

She opened her eyes and jerked her head back. "What? I never blush. Never mind. I changed my mind, I'll walk."

She stood from the bench and limped toward the exit of the park, with little needles stabbing her ankle with every step she took. Halfway, she slightly turned and shouted over her shoulder, "Can you take them? Thank you!"

Austin

Brennan

8

Brennan peered from the corner of his eye and had the privilege to witness a side of Errin she tried to hide above all.

She was gorgeous, as always. No doubt she still was the same proud and loud talking woman he came to know. But what drew his attention, and he sure did his best not to spoil the moment, was that for the very first time since he'd known her, she seemed vulnerable.

He wanted to park the truck, get her out of her seatbelt and put her little and lithe frame on his lap. He wanted to kiss that single tear away. The same tear she now stabbed away from her cheekbone.

He leaned over to her side of the Chevy and opened the glove compartment. With his eyes still focused on traffic, he rummaged around and took out the tissues. She grabbed them out of his outstretched hand but didn't voice thanks. Errin blew her nose.

They didn't talk on the ride over.

That bitchy receptionist, who later on appeared to be Errin's boss, fired her right on the spot. She shouted that the dog Errin lost sight of had run back on his own to the kennel and had been there for over an hour already.

While this Casey person was ranting at Errin, he stepped up

and demanded for the woman to shut her face. She had every right to be upset with Errin, to be mad at her even.

But the way she talked down to Errin, making snide remarks like she finally had the chance to go all out on her, had been unacceptable. She should have called Errin the moment that damn dog showed up at her doorstep. So he'd said as much before Errin put her hand on his bicep and steered him back towards the exit.

He heard that woman bitching while he stood outside on the sidewalk. Errin was irresponsible, never on time, and always had an attitude. Errin just hung her shoulders and asked him to take her to Lucky.

Not home, not to one of her sisters.

No, she wanted to go to Lucky.

His heartbeat had picked up knowing she wanted to spend time with him after being fired. She probably was going with him in the hopes she could talk with his grandfather, but he would take it, anyway.

He parked his black Chevy truck near the back entrance of the pub and opened Errin's door for her. She must have lost her spirit somewhere along the way, as she complied when he picked her up and walked her through the pub and directly upstairs to his apartment.

Normally, Errin would bristle at his assumption to take her to his place without even asking first. But not today—not now. He glanced down to take her in as he held her in his arms.

Her hair still had that warm, glossy hue to it, but the rest of her was fucked up. And even then she was disheveled into nothing but perfection.

Tears marked her freckled and rosy cheekbones. Her baby blues were red rimmed, just like her nostrils from blowing her nose. She had the ugliest, ill-fitting jeans on and a blue sweater with several holes in it. And to be honest, she reeked of dogs.

Everything that makes Errin this perfect angelic little spitfire was hidden by ugly clothing or tainted by her crying. But to him, she'd never been more beautiful. He entered his apartment, placed her crutch against the wall, and locked the door behind him. She remained silent.

He pushed his luck further by taking her into his bedroom. Her eyes widened in recognition and she squirmed in his arms. He held on to her tightly, not wanting to let her fall on the floor and hurt her ankle any more.

"Set me down, you ape! Don't know what you're thinking we'll do, but you can forget about it!"

He snickered as he placed her in the middle of his king-size bed. He was a big ass man and although his bed was a bit too big for the room; he didn't have the need for a lot of other furniture or any other belongings.

"Let me take care of you, Errin," he softly said. He was hoping to let her rest her ankle for a few hours since it was twice its size again. And okay, having her close to check up on her and help her find her bearings after this shit of a morning didn't sound too bad as well.

"Oh, you wanna fuck? Is that what you mean by taking care of me? You think because we had phone sex once, you can take me to your apartment? To your bed, to screw each other's brains out?"

He leaned in and she scooted back in retreat. He placed his knee on the side of the bed and placed his under arm next to Errin's head as she fell to the mattress at his approach. Her breath tickled his face. She was breathing hard, like a cornered animal ready to pounce.

"It's nothing like that, baby girl. Oh, but I do want you. I can't stop thinking about all the ways I want to fuck your big fuckin' attitude into submission."

Her eyes widened and narrowed just as quickly as she

scoffed. "Ha! Good luck with that. In case you failed to notice, I'm not some meek little mouse that will beg you for *anything*."

He chuckled. "Oh, I will have you begging, Lips. And soon."

"Cut it out with the stupid nickname! I hate it!"

"But it suits you. I can't think of anything better to call you." He laughed as she wriggled under him. She slammed her fists at his chest hanging above her, making it easy for him to take her wrists in his hands, placing them over her head against the mattress.

"You want me to bring out this defiant side of you. I think you like it a whole lot better than me seeing the vulnerable little Errin who's scared to let people see the real her."

Errin flexed her fingers and drew them into fists. She shook her head.

"But let me tell you this. As much as you haunt me with your perfect hot little mouth, dirty talks and sending half naked pictures of that banging body... nothing and I mean *nothing* compares to the shy smile you gave me earlier in the park. Or the way you let me bring you back here, after that shit storm of a morning."

She blinked and swallowed back a tear—unsuccessfully. He leaned in and kissed the tear away from her cheek.

"Thank you for letting me take care of you," he whispered against her ear before he got up and walked out of his bedroom.

He put the kettle on for tea. As he rummaged around, he tried to be vigilant in case she was trying to escape his room. But when no sound came from his bedroom, it made him antsy.

He placed a tray with two mugs of herbal tea, along with a cookie jar on his dresser. The shower started running in his attached bathroom and he walked over to his bed where beside it laid a pile of her clothes.

He picked the bundle up from the floor and her moss green lacy underwear drew his attention. While rubbing the delicate fabric between his thumb and index finger, he groaned as the only thing standing between him and a stark naked Errin was a bathroom door.

He counted to ten in his head and walked out to the hallway where he had a tiny side room for the washer and dryer.

After starting the washer for her clothes, he placed his ear against his bedroom door. The water had stopped running and Errin's singing in his shower stall filled his apartment.

He couldn't make out the song, but a smile crept up, and he placed his hand longingly next to his head against the door.

What was he to do now? She needed someone to take care of her, and not in the way she'd accused him. The thought of having his way with her entered his mind as soon as he saw her on top of his bed. Hey, he was a man after all.

But his goal was to let her rest her ankle for a day. Even for the night, if that's what it took for her to heal. Her stubborn arse would get pampered whether she liked it.

"Are you done creeping at the door? Are you lurking through the peephole, you perv?" she said with a hint of a smile in her voice. Hmm, the shower had done her some good. He knocked on the door, and when she didn't respond, he cracked the door. *Damn stubborn woman.*

"Why bother knocking, if you're still going to enter, anyway?"

She sat in the middle of his bed, with her back against the wall. She'd pulled the covers over her legs, up to her waist. And here she was again, the challenging Errin.

She was naked from the waist up, with her chest jutted out. Her lips curled, and she refused to break eye contact once his eyes landed on hers.

"Stop trying to distract me with sex, Errin. I just want to help you," he said, almost disappointed by walking in on her lying buck naked in his bed.

What the hell was wrong with him? Normally, a naked

woman in his bed didn't make him nervous. She narrowed her light blue orbs that sparked with judgment, since he wouldn't budge.

She crossed her arms under her perky tits, putting those hard peaks even more on display. What he wouldn't do to take her nipples one by one into his hot mouth. But he was ready for the challenge she just handed him on a silver platter.

He walked over to his closet and grabbed a white T-shirt from the middle shelf. When he turned, she had lost some of her bravado, hiding her breasts beneath the sheet. A cute blush crept up over her chest and colored her cheeks. Brennan handed her the T-shirt and turned around for her to put it on over her head.

She cleared her throat. "You can turn around now," she whispered.

"Okay, so scoot over a bit? Give my big ape butt a little room?"

She peeked up at him, puzzled, but did as he asked. When he sat down next to her, he deliberately sat on top of the covers. Errin didn't move.

He tucked a honey blonde strand behind her ear. "What are you thinking over there?"

She tilted her head and rested her cheek in his palm. Like a little kitten, she was eating up his touch and almost purred when he stroked her cheek with his thumb. She closed her eyes, stretching her long lashes over her high cheekbones.

When she opened her eyes, their striking blueness drew him in, making him forget all good intentions. He leaned in and she met him halfway. As their lips connected, he let his palm fall from her cheek and grabbed the back of her head to deepen the kiss.

As they kissed and kissed, she crept her hand under his sweater and onto his chest, making him shiver. He swept his tongue over her lips, and she opened up for him. A moan escaped him as her hand wandered over his chest to his side and she let her fingertips feather over his back.

"Errin..." he said between kisses.

She moaned in response and let the fingers from her other hand play with his black, wavy strands behind his ear.

"Bunny..."

She giggled, and he smiled against her lips.

"We have to stop kissing, baby girl. I don't want to go back on my word, and I always do as I promise. Let me take care of you, okay?" He pulled back and locked eyes with her.

"I've got some tea and cookies. You stay here in bed and let me pamper you, okay? Just... stay here and rest."

She bit her lip and smiled. Fuckin' cutest smile he'd ever seen. He'd figured she already gave *the smile* in the park earlier, but *this* was the smile he'd wanted from her all along, without a doubt.

"Bunny lass, where are ye girl?"

Errin smiled at Pops' booming voice from the hallway.

"I'm here, Pops. You can come in." She was dressed in Brennan's T-shirt and even stole his boxer briefs and sweatpants when he flew downstairs to open the bar at eleven. Her swollen ankle rested on top of a couple pillows.

"Ah, there ye are. I couldn't believe me own ears when me boyo told me. Stayin' the night again, eh?" he said while shuffling into the bedroom with a scrubby stool in his hand. He placed it beside the bed and parked his sizable frame on it.

His signature boisterous cough made her jump a little.

"You ever seen a doctor for that?" she asked.

"For what?" He shifted his colossal frame to catch her eye.

"For that sound you normally hear at SeaWorld." She smirked.

"Dunno ye talkin' 'bout?" he said.

"You know..." she said before she stretched her arms in front of her body, with her hands down and smacking her hands together while producing deafening short barks, "Oem, oem, oem."

His massive belly moved along as he shook with laughter.

"Aye, ye make a good seal. Can ye do any other animals? How bout doin' a turkey? Thanksgivin' is comin' up?"

She giggled and loved the fact he could one up her any time. She didn't put him off by her stupid jokes. No, he rather enjoyed them.

"What do turkeys do, then? Can you show me?" she said, smiling deviously.

Pops narrowed his green eyes mockingly at her and said, "Ha! I wasn't born yesterday, lass. I'm not goin' to gobble any time soon, ye hear?"

"Gobble?" she said.

"Yeah, gobble."

"What—"

"Not a chance in hell ye gettin' any gobbles outta me, lass." He then tilted his head as if it reminded him of something and added, "Unless... me boyo and Bunny lass are goin' to be wed. Then, and only on that day, Imma gobble the loudest gobble ye ever heard."

She shook her head laughing and eyed her foot propped up on the pillows. Pops cleared his throat.

"Ye know... I think yous a match made in Irish heaven. Yer like a filly, gallopin' the fresh green fields and he's the experienced stallion, showin' ye the way around the lands. Both can do with a bit from the other."

She'd never looked at it that way. Pops made it sound so simple, so natural even to be with his grandson. But what Brennan triggered inside of her was anything *but* simple.

He was out of her grasp, not easily manipulated by her usual means of distraction. He was tenacious, wanting to experience the *real Errin*.

And she did everything in her power to never let the real Errin out. She had no desire to show all her cards and bare her soul to him. This, whatever this was, wasn't leading up to anything. They couldn't differ any more. With him being the eleven years older, strong and silent type, and her, the loud and fickle type. He would run for the hills. So, why set herself up for heartbreak?

And then there's the whole moving back to Jersey plan. Although she didn't have the finances to go to any auditions there now, eventually she would try out again. Wasn't that the plan? Land a part in a professional production, move back home, settle in with Conner and slowly but surely pick up her old life.

She sighed. Yesterday, when they had phone sex, she'd figured they had their fun, and that was that. But this stubborn man had to bring up things like her smile, as if he'd figured out what made her tick.

He demanded to take care of her and didn't blink an eye, even turning her down while she sat buck naked in his bed. It gave her the impression he'd desired much more from her than she was offering. He may want her, but only on his terms. If he could get *all* of her.

"Whatcha thinkin' lass?"

Errin pulled on a thread from the covers next to her leg. She had to pick her words wisely. She's all too aware how Pops works: give him one finger and he would take her whole arm with it.

"I just don't know, Pops. He's your grandson and I—"

"He's me boyo and I love him to death. Yer me Bunny lass and I love ye to pieces as well. Imma keep rootin' for yous even though yer not there just yet. Just promise me to move it along a bit, I'm on me last leg here."

Errin snorted and said, "Ah, don't try to get any sympathy from me, old man. Nothing wrong with you, for sure."

He smiled knowingly, as he often liked to complain about his age even though he's as healthy as a horse, minus the cough.

"So, care to tell me what happened to ye?"

"I got fired from the kennel. I lost a job before, so it was nothing I haven't been through, and I hated working at that stinking place... but I guess I'm a bit at a loss right now. I miss the rest of my family, but whenever I stay with my brothers, I miss my sisters and vice versa. Pfff, and the last time I danced." She sighed. "I can't even remember the last time I had a gig."

Pops stroked his chin between his index finger and thumb while scrutinizing her ankle. "How long ye down for?"

"Just need to take things easy for a few more days. I needed that job at the kennel, so I went to work even though it wasn't the brightest thing to do for my recovery. It backfired in my face. Now I'm out of work and my ankle is the size of a watermelon."

He patted her leg. "To me, it shows yer work ethic is how it should be. Even though ye were down and out, ye still went in."

She shrugged.

"I want ye to work here at Lucky, Bunny lass."

She turned her head and snorted. "You've got to be joking."

"Nah, not jokin'. Yer perfect for the job." he waved his hand around the room as if it were ridiculous she didn't see it.

She laughed, but he didn't join her.

"Tell me how ye can't hold ye own with any situation or any person who may come at ye while working the bar," he said. "Tell me how ye hate to talk to random people, coming into the pub to share their life stories. Tell me how ye rather love a nine-to-five job, workin' behind a desk. Hmm?"

She let his words sink in. She'd worked part-time behind a bar a few years back and had been good at it. She'd quit working there because she'd landed a part in a dance production and couldn't combine the hours.

But working in the pub meant working alongside Brennan. And he was just the guy she wanted to avoid, at least for the foreseeable future.

Okay, she was staying here tonight and letting Brennan pamper her, as he'd called it. She wasn't going to bother Kayla or Kate, feeling like the third wheel while they were with their boyfriends.

Nobody else was around in her apartment, so she figured why not? But after tonight, they would go their separate way again.

"It's goin' to work out fine. Imma talk with Sean Jr. and I'll let ye recover for a few days. But then Brennan can work ye in behind the bar this Friday. Ye can start yer first shift on Saturday and start workin' yer Bunny magic around here."

She grinned at the Mills patriarch, knowing he was done with the subject. Whatever arguments she would bring to the table, he would sweep them all off. Working side by side with Brennan might not be sticking to her plan to avoid him after tonight. But with rent being due in three weeks' time, she figured she had to give this job a shot.

"Okay."

Pops nodded in satisfaction.

"Thanks Pops."

"Ah, no need thanking me, lass." He patted her leg once more.

"But if Brennan has a problem with me working at Lucky, I don't want to push this on him. I hope that you'll respect his wishes." Pops didn't respond, and Errin didn't like it one bit. "Pops..."

"Imma go to me boyo downstairs and grab me some lunch. Can I tell him to make somethin' for ye?"

"Yes, please. What are you having?" she asked.

"Full Irish, lass."

She laughed as that had to be the most stereotype dish for him to choose, as he was the only one around here who talked with a constant full Irish brogue. He quirked a brow and pointed at her.

"Ye can stop laughin' now, Bunny. Ye obviously hadn't had the Full Irish from me Emmy yet. She makes a mean fried eggs and sausage, I'll tell ye. It drags me out of me house for a reason."

"Is Emmy in today? Yes! Could you ask her to make me the usual?" Errin chortled as Pops quirked his brow.

"And what might me granddaughter be making for ye then?"

Pops' granddaughter Emmy, Brennan's cousin, started working as a chef for Lucky a few months ago and she and Errin directly hit it off. The stunning brunette gave back as good as Errin and she made a mean barmbrack.

"Toasted barmbrack, butter, the whole works, mmm." Errin's belly chose that moment to let out a growl, making them both laugh.

"Don't know where she got her talent from. Me daughter Shauni sure can't cook for her life."

"Did you teach Shauni?" Errin laughed.

"Pssht." The burly man dismissed the thought of him being a crummy cook.

"I've taught all me lads to cook a nice supper. But I'll tell ye, I have one daughter, and she burns down the house if you'd let her near a stove." He shook his head.

"How many kids do you have, Pops?"

Pops shifted on the poor stool that protested under his weight. The topic at hand made his features less grumpy as a hint of a smile tugged his lips.

"So, I've got one lass," he counted on his thick fingers, "Shauni. She has one son and five daughters. One of 'em is Emmy." He smirked as he said, "Ye know Sean Jr. of course, Brennan's dad."

He held up three fingers. "Then there's me son, Niall. He also lives in Austin. Has six kids and two of them work with him for his construction company. Ye'll meet them soon, they'll work with Brennan to fix up Lucky for us."

He chuckled as he added finger four and five. "And then I've got another two lads, living up in the mountains in Colorado."

"No way! You and Mrs. Mills sure liked to get around, eh?" Errin waggled her eyebrows.

"Ain't tellin' yer nosy arse nothin' 'bout that," he murmured, unsuccessfully masking the twinkle in his eyes.

Errin chuckled, putting her hands up in the air.

"But I know what ye mean, lass. I've got me so many grand-children. I think it's best if you take Brennan from me hands. And make it quick, will ye?" He winked at her.

She snorted and rolled her eyes.

"Brennan brought Emmy into the business and I'll tell ye, it's been his first decision for Lucky, but it will be one of the best," Pops said. "Emmy sure makes our hungry crowd happy. Imma tell her hi from ye and have Brennan bring something up."

"Thanks, Pops."

Pops left her to go down to the pub, and Errin hopped her way over to the bathroom. After doing her business, she used Brennan's toothbrush when there weren't any spares.

She spit out the toothpaste in the sink and let it wash away down the drain. She looked up in the mirror and met Brennan's heated stare.

He leaned against the bathroom door with his legs crossed at his ankles and his muscular arms folded in front of his broad chest. He'd put on a black 'The Lucky Irishman Pub' T-shirt and his black faded jeans clung to his tree trunk thighs.

She held her tongue—for once and stood motionless. She was gauging his mood as his nostrils flared and his stare made his green eyes blaze with fire. If she were a dutiful girl, she wouldn't poke the bear right now. But because she was Errin Walsh, she would do just that.

"You seem agitated, Bren," she said, eyes sparkling. "I'm sorry I took your clothes. Let me rectify the situation." Her fingers clasped the hem of the white T-shirt and she trailed it over her head. She'd forgone a bra, leaving her breasts exposed. The cloth dropped on the cold bathroom tiles next to her bare feet.

She held his stare in the mirror, drifting her fingers under the rolled waistband of the sweatpants. She slid both sweatpants and boxers over her hips and dropped them to the floor.

He eyed her, fully clothed from the bathroom doorway and licked his lips, eyes wandering over her reflection in the mirror. He stalked into the bathroom and locked the door behind him. She swallowed. The bear had officially been poked.

He grabbed her by the waist and she squealed in surprise when he hoisted her up and sat her down on the counter. She balanced herself by placing her palms on his pecs as he towered over her.

He leaned in. "I want you," he whispered.

She shivered. This beautiful, older man wanted her. And perhaps even *needed* her, going by the urgency in his whisper.

She licked behind his ear, and he groaned. His firm hands traveled from her knees up to her thighs. With precision, he nudged her legs apart for him to step into. He brought his hands to her butt and slid her to the edge of the counter.

With one hand to steady her, he used the other to open the cabinet above her head and grabbed a box of condoms. He snagged one and opened the package by tearing the foil with his teeth while staring into her eyes.

She leaned forward, almost falling from the edge but not quite. His belt buckle pressed against her belly and she shifted to maneuver her core straight against his crotch.

"Say you want me too," he said as he laid down the condom, still in the foil, next to her other thigh. He licked her closed lips and rocked his erection against her warmth. She mirrored his movements on instinct and from the friction alone she was almost ready for him to take her.

"Say it," he growled against her lips.

She held her tongue, although his tone aroused her even more. To showcase how easily she could match his fierceness, she finally kissed him back and then bit his lip.

"Ah, fuck!" he boomed. Their lips and tongues met in a frantic whirlwind, dueling for dominance. She wrapped her legs around his waist and pushed off from the counter, clinging to him. His hands found their way under her butt, pushing her close to him.

She ran her fingers through his hair and grabbed a firm hold of it. He roared as she yanked, tilting his head back to lick his throat. She was hungry for more and bit the side of his throat.

"Fuckin' wildcat. Yer goin' to be the end of me," he said.

Ah, he threw out the first 'ye's'. That was what she was going for. Get him all worked up and agitated so he'd talk in his delicious Irish accent. Hmmm, she loved angry sex. There was nothing better in her book.

"Stop talking," she bit out as she fisted his shirt. She tugged the shirt up and trailed her manicured pink nails over his chest, leaving marks for sure. He was licking her neck, but at her assault he nipped her.

"Aaah, yes, Bren! Yes!"

He launched her onto the counter and with one slick move, grabbed the back of his shirt over his shoulder and tugged it over his head. Beautiful. This powerful beast of a man would pounce on her as soon as he could free himself.

He opened the front of his jeans and took out his hard, long cock. Errin swallowed at the sight of it. She'd been with well-endowed guys before, but Brennan would outdo them all.

He grinned knowingly at her and fisted his dick before sheathing it with the condom. His index finger slipped from her outer lips inside her wetness as he tested her readiness.

"Get that hot pussy around my dick. Now," he demanded before taking his finger out.

She didn't need to be told twice.

She shifted from her seat on the counter, but he took control by lifting her under her armpits to propel her back into his arms. She clung to him like a little monkey and he directed her unto his hard rod. She slid down tentatively and bit her lip at his width.

Inch by delicious inch, he filled her while spreading her wider. The first throbbing sensations rocked her core, and she moaned out loud. "Ooooh yes, Bren. You feel so good."

"Fuck yeah," he said as he rocked. With every push and pull, his hard dick enticed her. And when he was inside of her, he was so deep, and he touched a part of her she never knew existed. His cock was made for fucking her. She was sure of it as it took only five pushes and she came from penetration alone. Well, that sure never had happened before.

He still pushed and pulled throughout her orgasm, making it last forever. "Oh. I... Bren..." she moaned and closed her eyes. She couldn't even think about being a smart ass right now.

She didn't even feel the need to run from him. At this moment, when he pleasured her into another world, she needed to take whatever he was giving. She longed for more of this ecstasy, so much more.

"I want you again, Bren," she breathed.

"What do ye mean again? Not done yet, baby girl," he said as he picked up his pace. In a menacing rhythm, he slammed inside of her while his balls slapped up against her butt. He took her by the waist and pushed her down against his jackhammering dick.

"You're even deeper. Fuck, Bren... I... I can't take it anymore." Her eyes rolled back in her head and droplets of sweat trailed over her temple. She was out of breath and tilted her head back as she came again. This time, no sound escaped her as the sensation overwhelmed her.

Brennan roared as he came. He grabbed the back of her head and pulled her to him to tongue fuck her again. She moaned against him, and he twitched inside of her.

"Oh my god, you're insatiable."

He grinned and kissed her once more before slipping out from under her. She deepened the kiss and pressed her hard nipples against his hairy chest. The soft hair tickled her hard peaks, and she arched her back to heighten the sensation.

"Yer so fuckin' hot," he said as he placed her back on the counter and took her nipple into his wet mouth. His swirling tongue plagued her, and she slipped a hand between her legs. When she almost reached her clit with two fingers, he grabbed her wrist.

He locked eyes with her and said in a raspy voice, "Gonna fuck yerself?"

"I..." She bit her bottom lip and smiled, unsure if he would go for that. Not every man liked for the woman he's fucking to get off by her own hand right after he pleasured her.

"That fuckin' smile right there. Fuck." He smiled as he directed her hand to her core. He took her nipple in between his thumb and index finger and rolled, then pinched it. Hard.

Errin found her spot, circling the hard little pearl repeatedly. Rubbing and pinching always did the trick for her and soon her legs shook with the inevitable release.

"Gorgeous. Fuck yerself. That's it." He moaned as he had

taken himself in his hand and apparently had taken off the condom to jerk off along with her.

His warm seed tickled her belly and when he smeared it into her skin around her belly button piercing, she almost wanted to lick his sticky fingers clean.

Ah, what the hell. She caught his wrist and swirled her tongue around his fingers.

"Yer so dirty, baby girl. I can't get enough of ye."

She giggled, his fingers still in her mouth, and eyed him through her eyelashes. He treated her with a goofy grin and kissed the tip of her nose.

"Perfect."

Austin

Brennan

10

"Em, I need a number ten and two twelve's for table six. And can you please reheat this for Errin?" Brennan asked as he pushed his body through the swinging doors of Lucky's kitchen, bringing Errin's untouched plate over to Emmy, who raised her brow.

He had a small spring in his step, walking over to the industrial-sized dishwasher. After filling it with dirty dishes from the lunch crowd, he closed the door at eye-level. He spotted his own stupid grin in the stainless steel door and wasn't bothered by it —not one bit.

He'd meant to take things slow with Errin, but when he brought her lunch up and walked in on her in his bathroom, he'd lost it. Errin brushing her teeth in his oversized sweatpants, rolled up at her tiny waist and her hair mussed like she'd already been thoroughly fucked made him disregard all reason.

The sex with Errin was everything he'd imagined it to be and then some. Oh, and he sure had his hot fantasies about Errin ever since their phone sex.

Just as he'd expected, she'd been eager, wild, passionate and so full of that fuckin' sass. He shook his smiling face and cleared his throat.

"Okay, Cuz. You've got to tell me something here," Emmy

said while crossing her arms in front of her white double-breasted jacket.

"What?" he asked as he turned to face his younger cousin.

"How come I made barmbrack and a Full Irish for Errin..." she glanced theatrically on her watch, "an hour ago, and now you're standing here, *in my kitchen*, telling me to reheat this plate?"

Brennan groaned, but nothing could take him out of his excellent mood, not even Emmy mouthing off and claiming her territory.

"*Your* kitchen?" He chuckled.

"Yes. Why can't you reheat it upstairs?" Emmy jerked her chin at his plate, making some shiny brown strands of hair fall before her eyes.

She pushed them behind her ear and continued, "You think I've got nothing else to do? That I'm sitting on my thumbs here? Waiting for you to come up with perfectly cooked meals and ask me to cook them twice? And rid it from all flavor, on top of things?" She placed her fists on her hips.

Brennan let out an exasperated breath and said, "Believe me, if I stayed upstairs to heat the damn plate, I might never come back down today."

Pops entered the kitchen and grinned while eyeing Brennan's still full plate. "Aye, Emmy. Yer giving me boyo yer piece of mind again? Don't go too hard on him, 'cause I think there's a perfect explanation this plate has been untouched, eh boyo?"

"Pops..." Brennan sighed.

"No, no, Imma say nothin' else. I swear." He held up his hand and spoke with the biggest grin he'd ever seen on his grandfather's face. Emmy raised her brow and glanced from Pops to Brennan. The tiniest smile flashed over her face before she cleared her throat.

"I see... Well, I'll do my best since it's for my girl Errin," Emmy said.

"I'm proud of ye, Brennan, me boy. Now, ye make sure ye hang onto hurricane Errin, ye hear? Let her sweep ye off yer feet and swirl ye around. Let her take ye to places yer never been, make ye feel things ye never felt before. Enjoy the fresh wind on yer face, take it all in and breathe..." Pops spoke as he spread his arms and took a big breath himself while closing his eyes for emphasis.

Emmy giggled above the stove as she cracked another egg on the edge of the frying pan. "Pops, never knew you to be such a hopeless romantic."

"Yer not in yer right mind if yer not romantic, lass. Nothin' hopeless 'bout that."

Sean Jr. entered the kitchen and laughed at his father's words. "I think my sister Shauni already has her work cut out to fend all those boys away from Emmy and her four sisters without them girls going all romantic."

Pops laughed, "Aye, yer forgettin' Emmy's brother Ryan. He'll fend them boys away all right."

"My mom wants a zillion grandbabies of her own ever since she's seen our cousin Keenan with his little Tommy," Emmy said. "I hate to burst her bubble, but I kinda need a man for that. Well, at least for the impregnation part."

Brennan snorted as he shook his head. Emmy shuffled the sausage in the pan and after the toast popped up, she picked it out of the toaster and put it on a clean plate. After setting all items in place, she handed the plate over to Brennan.

"I hope you'll let her eat this time," she said with a wink.

"What am I missing here?" Sean Jr. asked.

Brennan had no intention at all to talk about Errin with his dad, of all people. So he ignored his question. But the apple didn't fall too far from the tree as Sean Jr. kept on pushing, "Well?"

"I think another one of ye boyo's found himself a good Irish lass, son," Pops said with pride shining through his words.

"Ah. Another one bites the dust then, eh? Who is it? And am I soon to expect some grandchildren too?" Sean Jr. tried to nudge Brennan's shoulder with his knuckles, but he sidestepped his father just in time.

Sean Jr. cleared his throat and addressed Pops to change the subject. "I gave Errin the application forms, and she already filled them in. Errin and Lucky will be a perfect match for sure. Good thinking—"

"What the hell ye talkin' 'bout?" Brennan bristled as he turned to his father.

Pops stepped in between them and Emmy turned off the stove, keeping a close eye on the three Mills men.

"What got yer panties in a twist, son?" Sean Jr. boomed at Brennan.

"Don't call me that. You know I hate it when you act all fatherly all of the sudden." Brennan took a step closer with his chest puffed out. Sean Jr. winced but wasn't thrown by his son's words. Brennan stopped walking when Pops held his hand up, hurt marring his old wrinkled eyes.

"Boyo, take a deep breath. It's not Sean Jr.'s fault. I told Errin she could work for us."

Brennan took a step back and eyed his grandfather. He swallowed whatever curse came surfacing and blinked a few times. He glanced over at Emmy, but she shrugged behind the stove.

His eyes met his grandfather's, who nodded before adding, "I talked to her this mornin'. The lass needs a job, we have an opening—so she's goin' to work for us."

"Ye don't even know if she can work in a pub!" Brennan raised his voice but winced at Pop's stern look.

"Sorry, Pops," he said.

His grandfather hummed and said, "Nothin' wrong with Bunny workin' for us, boyo. Keep yer lass close, I say."

"Whoa, you were talking 'bout Errin earlier?" Sean Jr. said.

"Yes, *Dad*," Brennan said as he still couldn't let go of a lot of anger toward his father.

"For goodness' sake, cut it out, Brennan," Pops said. "Yer thirty-seven. Time to let the past sit in the past and let go of all this damn anger."

Brennan barreled out of the kitchen without replying to his grandfather and ran up the stairs to his apartment two steps at a time. This couldn't be happening. Just his luck that the moment he'd let his guard down and experienced Errin on a deeper level, she would end up working for him.

He wasn't following his father's footsteps in screwing his co-workers at Lucky. No way.

As he opened the door to his bedroom, Errin welcomed him, sprawled naked in his bed and giving him a lazy smile.

"Fuck," he said as he immediately closed the door again.

Errin giggled on the other side and said, "What are you standing behind that door for? Nothing here you haven't already seen?"

He leaned his forehead against the door and laid his palm next to his head. He counted till three before he spoke. "Did my father also walk in on ye naked arse?"

She bristled and said, "Of course not! You know I was completely dressed when you left for the kitchen earlier."

"Errin, I need you to get dressed again. Can you do that for me, please?"

"What? Why?" she said.

He sighed and cracked the door to peek into the room. She still laid in bed, but now with her arms over her bare chest, her chin jutted out and her head cocked to the side. Her nostrils flared as she waited for his answer.

"I... I need to talk to you. I can't concentrate when you're naked."

She scoffed at his answer. She swung her legs from under the sheet, over the edge of the bed. She hopped her nice and tight ass over to his closet to pick another of his T-shirts to wear. He stretched over to a stool next to the bed and waited for her.

After she put on a T-shirt that fell to her knees, she grimaced as she did her best to walk over with semi-determined steps. She sat as far away from him as possible on the bed, flattened her lips and nudged her chin toward him. "So, speak. What did you need to say to me?"

He took a deep breath, but she kept on talking. "Did you want to tell me, thanks for the fuck, but no thanks to another round?"

He growled at her assumption, but he let her get things off her chest first.

"Well, am I wrong here?" she said as she put her closed fists on top of the bed next to her thighs.

"No—"

"I see," she said and perched herself from the bed.

"No, you don't understand—" he said.

"Oh, I understand things perfectly, Brennan. Don't worry about me. I guess we had our fun and now it's over. No problem. Can you tell me where my clothes are?" she glanced around the floor in search of her clothes.

"I've washed them. Wait a sec. I'll grab them for you." He stood from the stool and winced as Errin sniffled when he walked into the hallway. Fuck. He needed to talk to her without fucking this all up.

He handed her the dry clothes upon entering his bedroom. "Thanks," she whispered. She hadn't been crying, but her trembling chin took him off guard. Errin was always in control of her emotions, so her struggle not to cry was kind of hard to watch.

"Errin..."

But she shot up her hand and said, "No. Please don't make matters worse. You did nothing wrong. I have one-night stands all the time, I should've known that this didn't mean—"

"Stop it right there, Lips." The thought of Errin with other guys angered him. He snagged her clothes back from her hands and planted them on the foot of his bed.

He engulfed her small hands in his and locked his green eyes with her baby blues. Her eyes drifted away over his shoulder, but he squeezed her hands once to gain her attention again.

"I just found out you'll be working for me. And I... I can't do this," he said as he waved his hand between them, "if I'm going to be your boss. In a few weeks' time I will run Lucky and I can't do anything to jeopardize that. I hope you'll understand?"

She didn't respond, so he continued, "But if you *wouldn't* work for me then—"

"Ah for fuck's sake, Brennan. Man the fuck up, will you?" Errin bristled as she jerked her hands from his to shove his chest.

He took a small step back in surprise and she placed her hands on her hips, daring him to come any closer again. "I really can't be bothered with your shit story." She poked her index finger in his chest.

He shook his head and took a step closer to her, but she held her ground and placed her palm on his chest.

"If you can turn your back so easily, right after what we did just an hour ago... you got another thing coming if you think I'll throw away a job opportunity for you now. Thanks for the offer, but no thanks. See you at work, *boss*."

She took her pile of clothing from the foot of the bed and

sidestepped him on her way to the bathroom. She slammed the door shut and locked it behind her.

Brennan took the bridge of his nose between his thumb and index finger.

"What the hell?" he whispered.

Austin

Errin
11

"I'm sure she's moping around here somewhere."

Errin looked over her shoulder from the downward dog position on her gym mat in the living room.

A zen voice from the television directed Errin to change positions and take a deep breath in between. That was all good, but first Errin needed to set her sister straight.

"Moping? No way, sis!" Errin shouted to Kayla who held her step in the doorway to the living room, causing Kate to bump into her from behind.

"Hi, Bunny. We just wanted to see how you're doing, after last night working with Brennan," Kate said over Kayla's shoulder.

"Yeah, yeah. Everything's fine. Just *fine*. Okay?"

Errin resumed her workout on the gym mat and tried another position, while her sisters took a seat on the sofa next to her. Holding on to her candle pose wasn't easy with four eyes following her every move.

"What?!" Errin ultimately shouted.

"Okay, sunshine. Namaste," Kayla said and snickered.

Errin let her legs fall down on the mat and huffed a breath. She peered through some loose strands in front of her face and winced at Kate's worried expression.

She should've known that after her first shift at Lucky last night, her sisters would check up on her. "Sorry. Didn't mean to be such a bitch," Errin said.

"We're used to it," Kate said.

After a second, the three sisters broke out in laughter since it was out of character for Kate to deadpan. Usually the roles were reversed.

"Donovan sure is rubbing off on you, sis," Kayla said while giving Kate's shoulder a playful shove with her own.

"Yeah, alternating between rubbing off on her and simply rubbing on her," Errin said, causing Kate's cheeks to turn an even darker shade of red.

"You make my boss sound like a dog in heat," Kayla said.

"And? Your point is?" Errin shrugged and laughed at Kate's uneasiness, as she'd rather not talk about all the hot sex she and Donovan were having.

Well, too bad the walls in this apartment spoke for themselves. Errin had the misfortune to overhear them multiple times in the beginning of their relationship. Yuck.

Kate cleared her throat and changed topics. "I've got an old smart phone for you. I think you'll like it better than the one you've got now as a replacement. It's in my bottom drawer. Mmm, at least I think it's here somewhere..." she tapped her chin with a finger.

"Or it's at your actual home, you know, with Donovan," Errin said. She straightened up from the mat to walk over to the kitchen.

"What crawled up your yoga mat? Let Kate be. She's happy with Don," Kayla said.

Kate adverted her eyes and kept them on a spot at the coffee table in front of her. Shit. Errin walked over to the sofa, almost hanging upside down over the backrest, to smack a kiss on Kate's cheek.

"I'm an idiot. Sorry. If you could lend me your old phone, that'll be awesome."

Kate patted Errin's cheek, already forgiving her. "You can have it, sis. No problem. So, how did it go last night?"

As Errin rounded the kitchen counter, she raised her voice a bit to make sure her sisters heard her loud and clear, in more ways than one.

"I've got nothing to report. I've worked behind a bar before. Everything's just the same. It's an Irish pub with a vibe as to be expected. Except for Emmy, who sure makes the most delicious food. I will get zero callbacks on my next auditions because they'll have to roll me off the stage."

They laughed. "It was fun. The Saturday night party crowd came in after Emmy closed the kitchen. I concocted a lot of new mixed drinks, had a few laughs with the regulars and hung out with some Mills brothers."

After closing the fridge, she was just in time to spy the look being shared between her sisters. She grabbed her water bottle from the kitchen counter and placed it back into the fridge. Instead, she chose an already opened bottle of wine. On her way back to the living room, she grabbed three wine glasses by the stems.

"Bunny! It's not even three 'o'clock," Kate said.

"Well? I'm free for the rest of the day." Errin shrugged.

"Brennan scheduled me to go back in on Tuesday. We're free to do what we want. You're both here, I'm here and lookie here... This wine bottle is here too." Errin waved said wine bottle in the air before placing the glasses on the coffee table and almost filling them to the brim.

"Well, it *has* been too long since we've had some sis-time." Kayla scooted to the edge of the sofa and threw her waist long silver blonde hair over her shoulder.

Errin grinned at Kayla as she took a glass and saluted them

before taking a hefty gulp. "Mmm. I've missed this, you guys," Kayla said.

Errin took a glass before sitting down next to Kayla.

"Yeah, me too. Cheers."

The cold wine didn't lessen her thirst from her yoga exercise, but that didn't stop her from downing her glass in a few swallows. Kate's eyes widened when Errin clanged her empty glass on the coffee table.

"Oh my God." Kate giggled, leaning forward to take the last filled glass from the table. Her long, silk brown hair partially fell from her back, sliding over her shoulder to the front. She took a sip and closed her blue eyes to savor the taste.

"Okay. Time to spill the tea." Kayla placed her half empty glass next to Errin's before refilling them. Her hazel eyes locked with Errin's, urging her to talk.

Errin took her newly filled glass and settled back on the couch. She placed her bare feet on the coffee table, daring Kate to comment on her nasty habit like she used to when she'd actually lived here. Kate averted her eyes and took another sip.

"Okay. I'll tell you the tea. You know how Brennan screwed my brains out a couple of days ago. How he was all like, 'let me take care of you' one minute and in the next 'you can't work for me if you still want my dick'."

Kate choked on her wine, followed by several loud coughs. She pounded her small fist against her chest while clearing her throat. "Bunny...."

"Yeah well, it is what it is. Can't say I regret fucking the guy. It was the best I've ever had—by far."

Kayla laughed wholeheartedly. "Sounds like a true Mills man."

Kate held up her hand to signal it had been too much information.

"And on top of things, Theresa called today. She has three auditions lined up for me in Jersey." Errin sighed.

Kayla furrowed her brows in confusion. "Why does that suck? You've been meaning to move back out there for weeks now?"

"I think Bunny might want to see what's between her and Brennan," Kate said before taking another sip.

Kayla shook her head. "Nah, Bunny wouldn't put Brennan above auditioning, that—"

"Aaargh." With a flair for theatrics, Errin threw her arms above her head.

"What? You told me yourself you wanted nothing to do with him anymore," Kayla said and leaned in to grab the almost empty wine bottle. After neatly dividing the last drops between the three glasses, she said, "Dunc said they never seen Brennan like this. He's even short with Pops."

"Nah, that's just him being an asshole," Errin said as she jutted her chin stubbornly.

"He still wants you, Bunny. It's plastered all over his face whenever you pass him by in the pub. His eyes were all over you when he was working you in on Friday," Kayla said before saluting her with her newly filled wine glass.

"Okay, the attraction is still there. I'll give you that. But I'm never going back there. Especially since I might head back to Jersey in a couple of weeks to audition."

Kate reached over Kayla's lap and took Errin's hand in hers. She squeezed once and said, "I'm sorry you're so homesick. If it hadn't been for me—"

"Ah, no. Stop it right there. I've never seen you, or Kayla for that matter, happier than you've been here, with your Mills men. When people fall in love, they tend to forget everyone and everything around them. And I guess it's time for me to make some grown up decisions for myself."

"Like?" Kate whispered.

"I'll do one last round of auditioning. If I make it, I will give it my all. But if it doesn't work out, I'm going to figure out what the hell I'll do with my life instead."

"Whatever you do, sis, we're here for you." Kayla patted Errin's knee before getting up from the sofa and strutting to the kitchen. "How about another drink, eh?"

Kate cleared her throat and shifted in her seat. She looked up at Errin from under her eyelashes and said, "Are you really moving back home? I mean... I would miss you like crazy. I miss you now, even though we're only a few miles apart whenever I stay at Don's place."

Errin scooted closer to Kate and placed her arm around her shoulder. "I miss you too, sis. But you already know that."

"Yes. I just wished that you and Brennan would—"

"Nah-ah. No, Kate." Errin shook her head. "I don't need Brennan to make me happy. And as much as I love you, I also don't need you here at the apartment to be happy. I think I'm just figuring this out."

Kate teared up, and Errin nudged her, ready to switch topics. "So. Enough of this emotional stuff. Can you find that old phone for me, please?"

Kate nodded and gave Errin a kiss on her cheek. "Love you, sis."

"Love you too," Errin said.

As soon as Kate left the room, Errin turned to Kayla.

"Can you call Donovan for me?"

Kayla blinked once before raising her brows. "Why?"

"Do it for me, please? He's your boss and will answer you," Errin said in a somewhat slurred voice. Damn. Downing that wine was catching up on her real quick.

"He would answer your calls too, Bunny. But I don't think it's smart to call him, since you just said you're suddenly all about making adult decisions..."

Errin clucked her tongue and held out her hand. Kayla shook her head while typing a few keys and handed over the phone. After two dialing tones, Donovan answered.

"Kayla? Something wrong? Where's Kate?"

"Donovan. Hey. Errin here," she started, but this alpha man wasn't impressed and asked again. "Where's Kate?"

"Geez. She's here. Nothing's wrong." She took a deep breath and had to fight the urge to roll her eyes.

"Okay. So, you're aware I can't handle alcohol, so please bear with me as I want to excuse myself in advance..."

Kayla groaned next to her and said, "Pff, this is gonna be good."

Errin shoved her shoulder in a playful manor. "Shut up, Kayla."

"Get to the point, Errin," Donovan barked in her ear. Errin never took to Don like she did to the other Mills men.

His dominance and aloofness rubbed her entirely the wrong way. Not to mention how he acted towards Kate in the first months after they'd moved to Austin to be reunited with Kayla.

She realized her sister wanted for Errin to act like it was all water under the bridge. But yeah, Errin never let go of anything.

Shit. Why am I even calling him? Oh yeah. Kate. She loves him. She's happy with the jerk.

"Okay. So just let me say this. I've been an absolute ass to you and Kate. You two deserve to be happy. I think she should move in with you. She obviously wants to, but she's just stalling because of me."

Kayla's placed a hand against her open mouth and above her hand, her eyes widened at Errin's confession.

"I mean it," Errin said and made a point of emphasizing this wasn't some drunken move on her part.

"I know you do," Donovan said.

"You do?" Errin furrowed her brows.

"Yes. You know how?" he said.

"Hmm, okay..." she looked over at Kayla in question, but since she wasn't on the phone with Donovan, she shrugged as to say she had no clue what was going on.

"Because I know you love her and how much she loves you. I've sat front row for these past months to see you both struggle with letting go. But Errin, you don't have to let go. Kate will never let you, anyway." They both chuckled, as it was true.

A few tears fell from her cheeks, darkening her gray yoga pants in the spots where they landed on her thighs. Kayla squeezed Errin's leg, making Errin cry some more.

"So. I figured that tonight, Kate stays here. We're getting drunk tonight," Errin held up her hand in reflex although he couldn't see her, but she was certain Donovan would interrupt her.

"Reeal drunk," she added, making Errin and Kayla giggle while sharing a mischievous look. "We're going to eat ice cream, do some stupid karaoke songs in the living room, and tomorrow, you'll pick her up to go to work. Okay?"

She didn't need to add that it would be Kate's last night in this apartment. They both knew the score.

Donovan cleared his throat and said, "Bunny..."

"Yeah?"

"Thank you. This mustn't be easy for you," he said.

"Yeah well... like you said, I love her," she said while locking eyes with Kate who'd just walked into the room, without the phone but with a questioning look on her face.

"Have fun, Bunny," he said.

"Oh, we will."

They hung up and Errin took hers and Kate's glass from the table and stood from her seat on the sofa.

"I would like to propose a toast," Errin said as she handed over Kate's glass.

"What's going on?" Kate said, looking between Errin and Kayla.

"Tonight, we're celebrating our last night as roommates." Errin held up her glass and Kayla joined her.

"W-what?" Kate said.

"Yep. Just hung up with Donovan. Tomorrow, he's going to pick you and your shit up, taking you home with him for good." Errin winked at a flustered Kate. Tears filled her eyes, holding a hand to her chest.

"Really?"

Kate's hopeful reply gave Errin a sting in her chest, realizing how wrong it was for her to guilt trip her sister in staying with her these last few weeks. It wasn't their fault Errin hadn't been as happy in Austin as her sisters.

She should've known the sweet Kate would put Errin's needs before her own, always thinking of others and asking nothing in return. She felt like a real asshole.

Kate cocked her head. "Are you sure?"

"One hundred percent." Errin nodded.

Kate stepped closer to Kayla and Errin, raised her glass and clinked it against theirs. Errin took a sip, almost choking on her wine as Kate took her by surprise by hugging her close.

"I love you," she whispered.

"I love you too," Errin said after swallowing her wine.

"What about me?" Kayla said.

"Always so needy. Pfft. Poor Duncan," Errin said with a smile in her voice before Kayla joined their hug.

"Shut up." Kayla laughed.

"Okay, enough of this mushy shit," Errin said. She broke away from their three-way hug and walked over to her television set up. "I want a battle against Kate. Pick your song, sis."

Austin

Brennan

12

"**B**rennan! Where's my refill?"

Brennan jerked his chin at Karl, a regular. Come rain or shine, Karl sat on the other side of the bar. When things were slow in the pub, Brennan couldn't avoid the idiot. Like now.

His father had a high tolerance and kept pouring the arsehole drinks even though he'd bitten more than he could chew. But opposite his father, Brennan wasn't your go with the flow kind of guy, and especially not with Karl.

It took some persuading his grandfather and father, but after looking over the stats and figures with them, Lucky is now closed on Mondays. It had been his second decision in his taking over Lucky in a few weeks.

The first decision had been hiring his cousin Emmy, and that worked out extremely well. But closing lucky on Mondays left Karl without a place to hang out and get his fix.

Brennan had thrown the middle-aged man out of the bar before, and his guess was this Tuesday would be one of these days.

The lady sitting next to Karl spilled her drink after Karl sagged against her elbow. "Karl, I told ye already. Ye had yer last one. No more tonight," Brennan said, mopping the bar with a wet towel.

It wasn't unusual to come across unhappy, angry or even depressed costumers on the other side of his bar. Often people tried to drown their sorrows with the help of the bottle, but they only made matters worse by doing so. He hated this side of his job.

"Never in the twenty years of coming here, I've been treated like this. You think you're better than me?" Karl spit.

Brennan glanced over his shoulder, just to check if Errin was out of reach of Karl. He wouldn't hurt her on purpose, but just like the woman sitting next to him, Karl sure had his casualties along the way while being this obnoxiously drunk.

"Karl…"

Ed, one of the other regulars sitting a few barstools over, tried to calm the arsehole down. But as usual, he wouldn't listen to reason.

"No, Ed. The minute this boy takes over, the place'll go downhill," Karl slurred, trying to retake his seat on the barstool, but failing miserably. He stood a little taller after finding his balance and said, "I give it two months before Sean Jr. will be back to save what's left of our Lucky."

And that was Karl's problem right there. Sean Jr. would no longer step in to pour his ugly mug another drink, even though Brennan had cut him off.

Brennan was officially taking over Lucky from his dad right after the renovation of their family's pub, starting next week. Well, if Karl had a problem with it, he could fuck right off.

"Karl. Ye better go sleep it off. If ye don't go right now, I might remember all this tomorrow and ye'll be drinkin' nothin' but water in Lucky from now on." Brennan kept both palms flat on the dark wooden bar, leaning over to make his point come across.

"Screw you. I'm out of here. I'm going next door. Where they *do* know how to treat their loyal costumers." He turned his tall but disturbingly fragile frame to stumble toward the exit. He bumped into several people before he finally found the doorway.

Brennan jerked his head to the sound of Errin's laughter. She stood in the middle of the pub in Ed's arms. The bald man had a soft spot for the latest Lucky recruit and Errin didn't mind wrapping Ed around her little finger.

"Okay, let's do this!" Errin said.

Errin motioned to Jessica behind the bar to start the music. Jessica gave a thumbs up behind the stereo and the first horns and violins entered the pub. Ed shook with laughter while Errin tried to keep a straight face.

"Ed. No, be serious," she said. "You wanted me to teach you how to dance. So come on!"

Her eyes sparkled as she kept her arms strong and pulled on Ed's lumpy arms so his elbows lifted. "Okay. Ed, that's good. Now don't droop your shoulders. Keep your upper body grand and beautiful."

Some of the old guys at the bar busted out in laughter and one of them shouted, "Yeah, that's Ed for you; grand and beautiful."

Errin was undeterred and stepped around Ed's belly pooch.

"That's right. See." Errin's hands on his shoulders caused his normally hunched frame to straighten. Ed's tall top stood parallel to the ground, and he smiled at Maureen, Errin's neighbor and Pops' dear friend who'd shuffled over to get a closer look.

"I love this song, Errin. It's so royal," Maureen said as she tucked a gray hair back into her bun.

"I know, right? I love how it makes me feel. Like a flower in spring. Ready to blossom." Errin spread her arms over her head and swirled her supple frame like a ballerina. Brennan smiled at her enthusiasm.

And he wasn't the only one being struck by the Errin lightning bolt. Even the old guys at the bar who often resembled the heckling Statler and Waldorf from the Muppet Show, were all engrossed.

Her lithe body was stuck in a black Lucky shirt, sensible light blue jeans, and botched black sneakers. Her work attire wasn't spectacular in any way. But she oozed sensuality without even trying. He pictured her in her ballerina leotard from Halloween and had to shift his stance. The image alone got him hard.

He turned to shoot a glance at the music installation.

Strauss–The Blue Danube Waltz.

It wasn't often that Strauss dominated an evening at Lucky, if ever. He shook his grinning head and looked over at Ed and Errin, who were sort of gliding around the makeshift dance floor.

Although red in the face, with sweat running down his temples, Ed persevered and even smiled down at Errin as the couple took another turn. They almost bumped into the booth closest to the pool tables, but Errin guided them just in time back toward the bar.

Errin fixed her eyes over Ed's shoulder on Brennan, and his mouth went dry at the pure and insane perfection of Errin. It was like they were in a game of who would divert their gaze first.

He wouldn't break their stand-off. Those light blue eyes shone with laughter and mischief. He needed that. God, did he need some of her rays of sun in his life.

The way Errin kept pulling on his heartstrings made him uneasy. He needed to clear his head and take a breather.

"Are you okay?" Jessica asked, drawing his attention from Errin.

"Erm, you know what? I'll take a quick break out back. I'll be a few minutes."

Jessica nodded and walked away to take another order at the far end of the bar. He strode into the kitchen, almost walking straight into Paddy, the middle-aged cook who'd been helping Emmy.

"Sorry, Paddy."

Paddy shook his head and mumbled, "No worries, Brennan, me boy."

Emmy looked up from her pan that wafted some exceptional aromas around the kitchen. "Cuz, I need—"

Brennan held up his hand. "Not now, Emm."

He walked past her, through the backdoor and into the enclosed back ally behind Lucky. He plopped down on the bench, placed his elbows on his knees and held his head in between his palms. After taking a couple deep breaths, footsteps sounded his way.

Errin's eyes met his as she balanced herself with one hand against the wall behind his bench, causing the spark to simmer in the air between them. Shit.

"Sorry, I know you're on a break. But Jessica assured me she could handle it."

Errin perched herself next to him on the cramped bench and took a deep breath, just like he had a minute ago.

"I know you're busy, so I'll keep this short," she said.

"Errin, what's so important you have to leave Jessica tending the bar on her own?" Brennan said while staring at the concrete wall in front of them. He was short with her and purposely avoided eye contact.

Because if he'd look into those sparkling baby blues, he would pick her up, place her on his lap and kiss her stupid. He would forget about his rule not to date women working at Lucky. About his rules to never turn out like his father.

"Phhst. Nothing she can't handle. Ed and four of his buddies are the last ones in. They're practically nursing their drinks back to life. Ed's beer is almost older than I am."

He didn't respond and she added, "But do you know what's even staler than those beers out there?"

He sighed and shook his head before she said, "Karl's breath."

That drew out a chuckle from him. As the lengthy silence between them turned awkward, he risked a glance over his shoulder.

Her eyes traveled from his chest back up to his face and just before their eyes met, he fixed his gaze on the concrete wall.

Out of the corner of his eye, he watched her eyeing him. Was she still affected by him? Like he was by her? Or was she sizing him up for an argument since he acted like a royal arse?

"You know what? It can wait." She stood from the bench and walked back into the kitchen.

He trailed his hand over his face. Fuck. He wanted Errin. Why did he have to be such an arse to her? Would it really be that bad to give whatever simmered between them a chance? He sighed and looked up at the inky sky.

His dad may have been a loose cannon, going through one woman to the next in the late hours at Lucky. Brennan sure as hell wasn't walking in those footsteps. If Brennan would do this with Errin, he needed to be all in. He smiled at the thought of Pops' description of the warm blonde spitfire. Was he ready for hurricane Errin?

Errin

13

"**B**unny, can I please have a Screwdriver and a Watermelon Vodka?"

The watermelon drink had to be for Caitlin—it was her favorite, but the Screwdriver was a bit out of character for her sister. She quirked a brow at Kayla, who giggled in return.

"The Screwdriver is for Fianna. I'll have a white wine, please." Kayla said while glancing around the bar. "Is Brennan out?"

Errin had tried to steer clear of Brennan since their almost chat the other night.

"Yeah. He went over to Kate and Donovan's earlier. Said he was coming back soon. Did you need him for something?" she asked.

"No. Just wondering how things are between you two," Kayla asked.

"Everything is just hunky-dory, sis," Errin said as she stabbed a slice of orange on the brim of the Screwdriver's glass.

"Bunny..."

"No. I mean it. He wanted to keep things professional between us, so I'll keep my distance, all right," Errin said while stretching to grab some ice cubes from the ice bucket.

"Did you tell him about the auditions yet?" Kayla asked.

"No," Errin said as she mixed vodka with orange juice.

"Chickenshit."

Errin huffed a breath and groaned. "I know."

"Theresa called today, said there's this one audition where the director called her twice now and instructed her I needed to come. It's Harold, the director I've worked with before. A total jerk, but apparently he sees me for the leading female dancer. Theresa said it's practically mine for the taking."

"That's awesome, Bunny. I'll miss you so much." Kayla gave her a watery smile as she brought her wineglass to her lips. Errin patted her other hand on top of the bar and gave her a sister a loving wink.

"Well, it seems like a sure bet. But anything can happen in the world of dancing. He might go back on his word the moment he sees me waddling through the door." Errin said, making Kayla scoff.

"Shut up." Kayla said.

Her sister set down her glass. "When would you start there, Bunny?"

Errin kept her eyes on the bar and said, "Next week. The production already started, but the leading dancer broke her ankle. The director said he's not happy with his current understudy."

"So soon! You have to tell him, Bunny," Kayla said.

"I tried yesterday, but he wouldn't let me talk to him. He acted like a real jerk. Wouldn't look me in the eye and basically dismissed me. But I'll tell my boss soon, sis. I promise."

"*Boss?* So you've decided to never speak of his name ever again?" Kayla smirked over the rim of her glass, peering with her hazel eyes at Errin's reaction.

"Yep," Errin said while preparing the last drink for her sister. She fetched two straws from the container and placed them in each drink. "So, all done."

"Thanks. Put them on my tab, will you?" Kayla said with a grin.

"Of course. Planning to go all out tonight?" Errin smiled while stacking up empty glasses.

"Dunc is out with Declan and Ronan, leaving the coast clear for Fianna to come to Lucky tonight since Ro is somewhere else. Are you and Emmy still joining us?" Kayla's mischievous grin was contagious.

"Yeah. I'll be done in an hour. You think you'll still be standing by then?"

Kayla snorted. "Ha! I'm no lightweight like you, sis. You just try to keep up with us, and then we'll talk some more."

She winked as she took the three glasses between her two hands, sloshing the drinks all over her hands but continuing to their table across the pub.

"Hey, can I have a beer? And your phone number while you're at it?" a chuckling voice said from across the bar.

She wasn't aware of the man filling Kayla's spot at the bar, but now he'd gained her attention, he definitely deserved her undivided attention.

The man had dark brown hair, and a neatly trimmed beard covering his chiseled chin. It reminded her of Brennan who hadn't shaved since she'd started to work for his family's pub and damn him, but Brennan was even yummier with his stubble.

She had to tilt her head for a closer inspection because of the height of this guy. And where Kayla easily stood in the same spot; his broad shoulders crammed him in.

"Sure. Draft or...?" she pointed at Ed's beer bottle, who was sitting on a stool next to this handsome stranger.

"No, whatever Ed's having is fine, thanks," he said as he nodded his head at Ed, who lifted his index finger from the neck of his beer bottle in greeting.

Mmm, so he wasn't a stranger at Lucky, just a stranger to her. She grabbed a bottle from the fridge beneath the counter and opened it in front of him.

"Here you go. Anything else?" she asked and stood frozen in place, taken aback by his emerald eyes. He came across as a younger and definitely more carefree than Brennan, but somehow he still reminded her of Brennan.

"Well, I remember asking you for something else as well..." he said before taking a gulp of his beer.

She cleared her throat and rubbed her hands over her jean-clad thighs. "Well, okay. I can do that."

He raised his dark brows while the tip of his beer bottle still rested against his full lips. He hadn't counted on her giving in so easily. She took out a coaster to scribble her phone number on, but hesitated for a second.

Was she really giving this stranger her number? She went with a little white lie and said, "Oh shit. I forgot. My phone's broken."

He didn't have to know she'd got a replacement phone from Kate now did he? The handsome guy laughed with his head back and when he placed his twinkling eyes on her again, she couldn't stop a giggle escaping her lips.

"Okay. That's a new one for me," he said as he gave her a lopsided grin and tipped the beer bottle in cheers toward her.

"No, for real. A dog ate my phone—" she started, but he just kept on laughing.

"What's so funny here?" If Brennan's rumbling voice wasn't distracting enough, his manly scent was doing her in.

"Hey, Cuz. What's up?" the man said as he gave Brennan a man hug, leaning over the bar. They slapped each other's back and Errin shook her head after what he'd said dawned on her.

"Cuz?" she asked tentatively.

"Yes. This is my cousin Keenan. He'll work on Lucky's renovation," Brennan said, waving his hand toward Keenan.

"Keenan, meet our new employee, Errin."

She scoffed at his introduction. As if she was just his employee and nothing more. Well, perhaps that was all there was to it for him? She righted her shoulders and stuck out her hand for Keenan to take.

"Nice to meet you, Keenan. And if you'll excuse me, I'll find me a new phone so we'll be able to connect soon."

She winked at his smiling face before she slipped her hand from his firm grip, turned on her heel and burst through the swinging doors to the kitchen.

She closed her eyes and laid her hands on her stomach for a moment to breathe in as much oxygen as she could. Damn Brennan with his professional attitude.

"Ah, Errin! Finally. Is it time for our well-deserved drinks? Are the others still there?" Emmy said while cleaning up the last workstations for the night.

It was around eleven thirty and the last snacks just went out front. Emmy and the other kitchen staff, Paddy and Earnest, had been through a hectic night with a lot of backed-up orders when the stove broke.

Errin respected the hell out of Emmy, who drilled both middle-aged men to still bring everything out, working with one little portable gas burner left.

"Hey, yeah. Cait, Kayla and Fianna are waiting for us."

"Something wrong?" Emmy said.

"Nothin'. Just breathin'," Errin said with her eyes still closed. She peered through one eye when Emmy snorted.

"You're so weird," Emmy said on a chuckle.

"Well, it's the slogan of this city, ain't it? Keep Austin weird?" Errin responded as she grinned back at the cheeky brunette.

"Hmm. Yeah, I guess you're right." Emmy laughed.

"I can't wait to this shift to be over," Errin said as she folded her arms in front of her chest.

"Tell me about it. It's a good thing Brennan is renovating the pub. This kitchen is falling into pieces. I'm scared of opening the door to the freezer, afraid I'll end up with the entire thing in my hand," Emmy said as she blew some warm chestnut hair from her face that had escaped her high ponytail.

In the previous months, Errin and Emmy had shared a few drinks at Lucky in a group with Errin's sisters and a couple of Mills brothers. They even met up twice a week to take a yoga class together at Duncan's Dojo. But working alongside at the pub brought them vastly closer.

"Are you coming back out or what?" Brennan said with his head peeping from between the swinging doors. He dragged his hand through his hair before walking further into the kitchen. Emmy turned her back to them and wiped the counter on the far end of the kitchen.

"So. What's up? Are you hiding out for Keenan or something?" he asked while wiping his hands on the kitchen towel that hung near Errin's spot. Emmy snorted loud enough at his words for Errin and Brennan to both briefly glance her way.

"Keenan's here?" Emmy asked.

"I was just taking a break. I'm coming." Errin fake fluttered her eyelashes, mockingly sucking up to him as she said, "I'm sorry, boss."

"Cut it out, will ye?" Brennan said as he narrowed his eyes at her.

"Whatever do you mean?" Errin said.

"I fuckin' want ye to stop actin' like a child. Stop callin' me boss and start workin'," he bit at her.

"Well, I can do that. If you'll excuse me, *boss*?" she said before she tried to step away from him. He grabbed her bicep and leaned in to whisper in her ear, "Stop tryin' to get a rise out of me."

She closed her eyes and groaned out loud. "What do you want me to call you then? Because you were the one who declared you're nothing but a boss to me... so what's the deal here?"

Emmy cleared her throat and walked past them on her way to exit the kitchen. She called over her shoulder, "I'm going to see my cousin. See ya later!"

Errin stared into Brennan's eyes and said, "Yeah, okay, Emm..."

He waited for Errin to speak first. Probably so she'd play by his rules and let him get away with fucking her and discarding her within the hour. Well, he could wait a century for all she cared.

They were the only two in the kitchen now, and gazing into Brennan's eyes brought back flashbacks of his lips on hers over a week ago. She focused on his full lips and glanced back up into his eyes.

He studied her features attentively and the moment she closed her eyes, he tugged her by her bicep he still held on to and pulled her in close to his chest. His body was warm and rock solid.

His black Lucky shirt was just as smelly as hers, after chicken wings and spilled beer. The scent should repulse her, but it was starting to smell like home. Working at Lucky was feeling like home. *Shit.*

She didn't want to let him in again. He saw through her once before and she couldn't let it happen again. He could leave permanent scars on her heart if he was to ever come so close to her again and decide she wasn't good enough for him once more. She didn't trust him. He was the one who said he couldn't get enough of her. Said he wanted to take care of her one moment and in the next, treated her like crap.

She would leave next week to dance again in Jersey, anyway. What was the point in letting him rattle her? In letting her guard down? But he would have to keep his beautiful face away from her.

He just smelled too good. She'd often woken up late at night, dreaming of his words of passion breathed against her neck. And not only his words but also him marking her that morning still haunted her. She still had the bite marks to show for it, albeit fading.

"What's the difference between a waitress and a toilet?" she blurted, opening her eyes to meet his furrowed brows. He leaned in to look her in the eyes and said, "What ye talkin' 'bout?"

"A toilet is only expected to deal with one arsehole at a time," she said as she swiftly took a step back out of his arms and sidestepped him. She strode out of the kitchen, leaving the wooden swishing doors to move back and forth a few times because of her forcefulness. She had thirty minutes left of her shift and she would finish it, damn it.

Austin

Brennan

14

"Do you want some?" Brennan poured a glass of milk to calm his stomach. He often needed some after working a long shift. He put the carton back into the fridge the moment Don shook his head.

"Nah, man. I'm good. Just had dinner with Kate and Errin downstairs. Emmy fixed us a real nice plate. You did real good with hiring our cousin. Fuck. Who'd have thought a daughter of Shauni could cook like that? I remember spending one summer on their farm, sneaking aunt Shauni's home-cooked meals into napkins to feed the pigs with later on."

Brennan hummed but said nothing as his mind drifted to Errin and Emmy. 'The two spitfires of Lucky', Pops had renamed the duo. They both killed working at Lucky. Emmy in the kitchen and Errin out on the floor proved to be a unique but equally powerful duo.

The customers loved Emmy's food and therefore Lucky became more than just a bar to grab some greasy food next to your beer. She brought back some class to his joint. And Errin, — of course she killed it. He snorted.

"What?" Donovan asked while sitting down at the kitchen table. On top of his dark blue jeans, he wore his signature black button-down-shirt, with the sleeves rolled up over his elbows.

"You happy, bro?" Brennan asked.

"Yeah, B. Real fuckin' happy." Donovan snickered at his own words, not believing he'd said it out loud.

"Good," Brennan said. At least someone was fuckin' happy.

"Want to talk about it? We always come to you for advice, but you know you can talk to me, eh?" Donovan said before he grabbed Brennan's glass and downed half.

Brennan rolled his eyes and stood to pick another glass from the cupboard above the sink. Once he'd filled the glass, he sat opposite of his brother at the table. A few moments of silence passed, and Donovan was the first to break this weird tension that never used to surround them.

"Okay, ye know when ye came over to my apartment and spoke to me about Kate? How I fucked things up and how I needed to man the fuck up?" he started with his agitated Irish brogue.

"Don..."

"Don't ye 'Don' me, bro. Ye always had our backs. Ever since Ma died—"

Brennan stood from his chair and the shrill sound of his chair scooting back over the kitchen tiles pained his ears but worked wonders to silence his brother mid sentence.

Donovan stood as well and placed his open palms on top of the kitchen table while leaning in. "Sit back down and hear me out."

"The fuck I will." Brennan narrowed his eyes at his younger brother. Who was he to come in his home and tell him to sit down? *Fuck this shit.* He walked over to the couch and plopped down. He snatched his sneakers from under the coffee table and yanked on his shoelaces.

"Ye always had to take care of us. Makin' sure Ronan didn't get into another fight at school. Keepin' me in line when I was too busy chasin' tail and slacking on my homework. You were always keepin' the rest of us out of Dad's line of sight whenever he spent a night at home to play the part of a devoted father."

Brennan shook his head but held his hands still, listening to Donovan. What he said was true. Ever since their mother died of breast cancer, Sean Jr. couldn't handle the pressure of raising five sons in the ages between six and fourteen on his own. Not while working at Lucky all the time.

But even though his father had labeled Brennan in charge as oldest son, the outcome by his request, Sean Jr. never quite coped with the boys turning to Brennan.

The final straw for Brennan had been walking in on his dad when he was screwing some woman in this same apartment. Brennan had been eighteen at the time and took on a weekend job at Lucky.

He was drowning in the responsibilities at home, keeping barely afloat with the challenging Ronan who was at a path of war all the time. Ronan was always talking back and busting his balls whenever Brennan tried to guide him in the right direction.

And here his dad was, screwing his brains out and having the time of his life at their family's pub. Brennan hated him ever since. Brennan sighed and glanced over his shoulder as the couch next to him dipped under Donovan's weight.

"Talk," his brother said.

"Dunno man. Where to start?" He sat back against the couch. He stared up at the ceiling. "I can't stop thinkin' I made a mistake with Errin."

"By hiring her or by taking her to bed?"

Brennan turned to eye his brother.

"Or by cutting things off with her?" Donovan added as he cocked his head.

"Yeah. Well, she irritates me like no other. If she tells me one more stupid joke, I will lay her over my knee and spank that sass right out of her arse."

Donovan bellowed a laugh. "I like how you think, but good luck with that, B."

"You'd think she'd been born and raised in a bar, with all the filthy jokes she sprouts and the swearing and stuff. Nothing gets to her, Don. You know how the regulars try to test the fresh meat behind the bar. Ha! Errin told them to fuck off and smiled in their faces. And when Ed is done ogling her fine arse, another sucker comes up to the bar and tries to get in her pants."

"I swear if I see Keenan eyeing her one more time, I will knock him on his arse. For the last two days, he's been constantly here. Supposedly to do his research for the renovation, but he's always hanging around the bar, laughing like some kind of idiot."

Donovan snickered and held up his hands when Brennan glared at him.

"Do ye know who is even worse than Errin? Pops. He can't shut up about how I messed things up. Sayin' I need to step aside so Keenan can have a shot with Errin because she would make the perfect stepmom for Keenan's little boy Tommy."

He pursed his lips while his brother laughed again.

"Shut the fuck up, Don."

"Sorry man," Don said with no remorse. "It's just that you told me not so long ago you'd never gonna talk to me 'bout someone who—"

"Yeah, yeah. Stop yer fuckin' gloatin' already. I know I told yer arse that I don't do the whole love thing." He crossed his feet on top of the coffee table and swept a hand through his hair.

"And this is it? I mean, this a love thing?" Donovan probed.

Brennan took his time contemplating his brother's question. It was a fair question, but not one to answer without giving it a good thought. The spare moments they'd spent before all went to hell had been hands down the best he'd ever experienced with a woman.

Sure, he'd had girlfriends in the past, but none of them challenged him like Errin. Come to think of it, they'd never argued about anything, preferring him in charge.

But not Errin. She was elusive, always just out of reach and trying to change the rules along the way. This ball-buster was evermore ready to take him on. It made him step up and take notice of every single thing that made up Errin.

Although she tried very hard to deter him from her, he wanted nothing more than to break down that armor surrounding her heart.

"It can be," he finally offered.

"Then go after yer girl, man. Don't let Pops, Keenan, or any other guy stop ye from gettin' what ye deserve. And especially don't let yerself get in between yous two."

Brennan groaned, knowing what would come.

"Well, aren't ye tellin' yerself ye can't be with her because she's workin' for ye?" Donovan asked as he quirked his brow.

"Well, fuck that. Ye ain't nothin' like Sean Jr.. Not in a million years. Ye don't need to hold yerself to these damn high standards all the time. Nobody is ever goin' to compare ye to our old man."

Brennan closed his eyes and took a deep breath. Fuck. Talking about their past still hurt. Even after twenty years, he still tried to put as much distance between him and his father as possible. If he didn't love Pops as much as he did, he would have never even considered stepping one foot inside of Lucky.

The pub was part of the reason things had gone to shit between him and his dad. But it had also been the place where he first followed his grandfather around, watching his every move and mimicking him in his grumpy ways.

Pops would sit him on his lap to tell him the most intriguing stories that, he now realized, were made up from the beginning till the end. And later on, Pops was the only one who really listened to him, giving him advice about handling the boys, made him take no shit from no one.

Pops' disappointment in him was another thing weighing him down the past week and a half. His grandfather warned him to never hurt his Bunny lass. And did he listen?

There was a soft knock at the door and Kate pushed it open. She bit her lip before she took a slight step into the doorway. The chocolate haired Walsh sister cleared her throat before greeting them.

How did such a sweet, shy girl end up with his brother, the all-time player of Austin, Texas? Though, he'd never seen a more perfect match in his life, surprisingly enough.

"Hi. How's it going?" Brennan said.

"Uhm. Good, thanks. Eh, I... I figured we might go home?" she said to Don.

"What is it, Cupcake?" Donovan crossed the room and took her by the hand before leading her inside. She blushed, and Brennan couldn't help but snicker at the contrast between her and her younger sister Errin.

Errin walked into a room like she not only owned the place but also bought the place right from under your nose and made a big profit out of it. He grinned.

"Is something wrong?" he asked Kate.

She looked over between Don and him and said, "Erm, it's Errin. She's... well, she's celebrating, because you've paid three months rent for her...", "Erm, it's Errin. She's... well, she's celebrating, because you've paid three months rent for her..."

Brennan fastened the last shoelace while glancing over his shoulder. "You've paid her rent?"

"Well, I figured she hadn't been planning on living alone in her apartment. Because Kate's moving out was so last minute, I transferred the money this morning. But she more or less threw it in my face when I told her tonight."

Kate shifted her balance. "She didn't mean to sound ungrateful, Don. It's because she doesn't plan on staying in Austin. It's a real possibility she's leaving for Jersey next week."

"What?!" Brennan roared.

"Um... there's an audition in Jersey that seems to be a sure thing. The director called her agent—" But before the flustered Kate could elaborate, Brennan went downstairs to get his answers from the horse's mouth.

Errin's loud laughter traveled through the room when Brennan entered the pub. She sat at Pops' table near the bar. With fuckin' Keenan. A pitcher of beer stood between them on the tabletop, and several smaller shot glasses littered the rest of the table.

"Nah, Beautiful. Come on, don't chicken out now." Keenan poked Errin in the side.

Errin hiccupped and smiled over the rim of her half full shot glass. Brennan eyed his cousin's gaze wandering over Errin's tempting body. She sat on the worn wooden chair in a black halter dress that halted mid thigh over her crossed legs.

Her wavy hair fell down her back and her light blue eyes sparkled because of some cobalt blue eye make-up. Her red lips distracted him from her natural beauty. She hadn't worn this kind of make-up around him before, and she sure didn't need any of this stuff.

"What in the hell is goin' on here?" Brennan boomed as he towered over Errin, standing next to her chair. She swallowed the second half out of her shot glass and placed her Ferrari-red fingernails against her luscious red lips. Her doe eyes gazed up at him, and he detected the start of a brief smile.

"Hey, Cuz. We're just having some drinks. Wanna join us?"

Keenan smiled as if he wanted Brennan to play his juvenile drinking game with them.

What an arsehole his cousin was. If Brennan would be on a date with Errin, he sure as hell wouldn't go to her place of work. Let alone let another guy join them at their table.

"Sure." He smirked while taking a very close seat next to Errin. He laid his arm over the backrest of Errin's chair and eyeballed the competition. *Bring it the fuck on, sucker.*

Austin

Errin
15

What started out as having some innocent drinks with Keenan after her dinner with Kate and Don, escalated quickly into a cold war.

Maybe her vision wasn't all that clear after downing two shots with Keenan earlier, but the sudden icy atmosphere was killing the mood.

She glimpsed next to her, at Brennan who smirked at his cousin Keenan like a certified mad man. He was kinda scary with this big ass fake smile on his worried-lined face, above that sexy beard he just recently started sporting.

As always, she talked before thinking things through and blurted, "What's the difference between a G-Spot and a bottle of Jack Daniels?"

Brennan groaned next to her, but Keenan sprouted his beer all over the table.

"Fuck, didn't see that coming. At all." He said after wiping his face clean with a dark green napkin. Errin's eyes fixated on the yellow Lucky logo on top. She tried to focus, but her vision blurred.

Keenan took another couple of napkins and tried to wipe the table clean from his spilled beer. He shook his head, chuckling. "I'm kind of scared of hearing the answer."

Errin grinned and placed her hand on top of his as he wiped

the table. "No need to fear little 'ole me." She gave an exaggerated wink for emphasis. Brennan cleared his throat, and she suddenly remembered sitting at Pops' table at Lucky and instantly retreated her hand.

These two Mills cousins were in the middle of a stare down before she threw out the first joke that came to mind. With any luck, the ice would break between them and they all would get along.

She focused on Brennan when he rested his hand at the side of her neck, just under her jawline. Did he pick up on the fact that her heart suddenly increased its pumping as his fingers rested on her pulse? His thumb stroked the corner of her bottom lip, probably smearing her lipstick all over her face.

She tried to pull away, but he held her in place and locked his eyes on hers. In that exact moment, she was now certain of what she'd questioned these past days while working with him in the pub.

He wasn't over her. Just like she wasn't over him. He still cared. *Fuck him.*

"A guy will actually SEARCH for a bottle of Jack," she whispered.

Keenan snorted, but Brennan smiled at her. They both knew how much he hated her deflections. But he was on his way to get a little piece of her that no one ever held before. Maybe if he hadn't stomped all over that same heart, she would let him.

From the corner of her eye, she spotted Keenan rising from the table. But she didn't acknowledge him.

The bright green orbs in front of her mesmerized her, pinning her down to her seat. She couldn't move a muscle. She sat in the center of his attention and wanted to stay in the eye of this proverbially tornado storm forever.

"Tell me why you're leaving, Lips."

He knew? Who told him? Why? She wanted to be the one to tell him. Shit.

"Don't look so shocked. Or where you never going to tell me?" he said.

Her eyes narrowed, and she tried to jerk her cheek from his hand, but he didn't let her.

"If you'd let me talk to you out back a few days ago, I'd have already told you." She jutted her chin and dared him to argue.

"So it's true then? You're walking out? Leaving Lucky? *Leaving me?*" he said the last words while slamming his fist against his chest. Shit.

She shook her head to let his other hand fall down from her cheek. "Leaving *you*?"

"Yeah. Leaving *me*," he said.

Errin raised her voice, not caring they were sitting in the pub where everyone knew them and were without a doubt listening in. She waved her hands between them as if they could help her explain.

"There *is* no 'me leaving you', Bren. Do you know why? Because we're not together."

Brennan jerked back like she'd struck him.

"It's how *you* wanted it. Well, let's be apart, I say. Let's be apart with you in Texas and me in Jersey. See if I care!"

Her eyes remained frozen on his face as he stood from his seat. He held out his hand and kept his gaze on her.

She glanced around and sure enough, the whole pub was so quiet, you could hear a pin drop.

She waved his hand away, but stood up to walk to the back-door. He brought his warm hand to her lower back.

She walked up the same damned stairs that put her into this mess in the first place. He chuckled at her theatrical stomping in front of him.

She swirled around upon entering his living room. After

locking the door behind him, he grabbed the back of his gray T-shirt and tugged it over his head, giving her another glance at his defined abs and hard chest. She swallowed and let her eyes travel over the neatly trimmed hairs on his chest.

Although him stripping was unexpected, it was awfully tempting to take him up on his offer. Should she throw caution in the wind? She couldn't wait to scrape her nails over his back as he'd fucked her. But he'd better learn some ground rules beforehand. If she did this, it would be on her terms.

As his eyes traveled over the halter-top of her dress, she placed her hands on top of her hips. "Take me to bed, Bren. Hmm, and do it like the last time. Rough. Hard."

He licked his lips, and she held up her hand while she walked right up to him.

"But it's just a farewell fuck. After tonight, we're not doing this ever again. After tonight, we're done. You'll let me go. We're clear?"

His eyes blazed with fire as he toed his sneakers off. He took his black leather belt in his hands. After unbuckling it, he undid the first three buttons from his jeans and let it nonchalantly fall open.

The bulge under his black boxer briefs grabbed her attention. A throbbing sensation started between her legs in anticipation of what this beast of a man could do to her.

His entire demeanor changed after her words, and he said through gritted teeth, "Ye think yer the one callin' the shots here?"

She quirked a brow and scoffed at him. "You know I am. You may be my boss, but you're definitely not the boss of me outside of Lucky. Best you remember that."

This bulky man, strong with muscles upon muscles, wild and unruly raven hair, a similar dark beard and penetrating eyes, was trying to stare her down.

Would he let her set the rules so she could keep her emotional distance from him? Even though she needed this potential fuck as much as he did?

She needed closure. Working for him after his sudden dismissal had been frustrating. She didn't want to be attracted to him, but every shift her eyes kept searching the pub for him.

All unreciprocated flirts thrown his way at the bar, sparked a stupid hope inside of her. Maybe if she fucked him now, she could fuck him right out of her system too.

She had to try, because even spending the evening with the handsome Keenan didn't do it for her—at all. Sure, Keenan rocked that whole sexy-single-dad-thing.

How lovingly Keenan talked about his two-year-old son was cute as hell. But all she could think of when she gazed at Keenan in his emerald eyes was how they didn't match Brennan's.

She broke eye contact and glanced around his apartment. Two half full glasses of milk stood upon the kitchen table and she turned back to Brennan and cocked her head in question.

"Pops is at his place but Don stopped by. Kate was the one who told me what the fuck was going on," he said.

Errin swallowed back her response. She would give her sister a good talking to about blabbing about her business. "Where's my sister now?"

"She walked right past ye downstairs. Even tried to say hello to ye but ye were too busy eyefuckin' me cousin to acknowledge yer own sister."

He was trying to get a rise out of her. Well, if he tried a little harder, he could get fucked—without her. She narrowed her eyes at him but withheld any response at his accusation. That proved to be the wrong tactic as it agitated him more.

While taking off his jeans, boxer briefs and socks, he said, "Fuckin' had to watch him ogle ye. Watch him get hard for ye."

Her eyes widened and her eyebrows couldn't go any higher. *What the fuck?*

"This is the first and last time yer flirtin' in front of me. Yer goin' to make me fuckin' crazy if ye do. Can't have other men thinking they can get with ye."

With his clothes gone, his natural fragrance engulfed her and made her knees buckle. She remembered it as he'd pumped in and out of her in his bathroom. His scent had surrounded her all over that day he brought her back from the kennel, when she laid in his bed and he'd kissed her.

"This is just a fuck," she said into the air to remind them both.

She moaned as he caressed her collarbone with sweet kisses. He reached out and held her zipper on the back of her black dress between his fingers. She wobbled in her high heels, but he embraced her with his powerful arms, pressing his erection against her belly.

The zipper went down at a treacherously slow pace, but he didn't pull the wool over her eyes by doing things leisurely. It was the quiet before the storm. She gazed into his eyes and witnessed his anger battling his lust.

"You want me. No matter what ye say 'bout farewell fucks and all that shite."

Before she could argue about this being their last fuck and nothing more, he took the hem from her dress and lifted it up, over her hips, over her waist, her small and now naked breasts and ultimately over her head.

The dress fell to the floor, and he stroked the apple of her cheek while she leaned into his touch. His predatory smirk almost had her sighing in defeat, as he might as well do with her as he pleased by now.

But as if struck by lightning, she jerked her head from his hand. *I'm Errin fucking Walsh.* He narrowed his eyes in annoyance and placed said hand on her hip. His index finger slipped under the silk, metallic colored fabric and tugged it over her hip, letting it rest mid thigh. She tried to take a step back, but he held her in position.

"Yer like a wild filly. I don't wanna spook ye," he said as he took a few loose strands with his other hand and placed them behind her ear.

"You just want to tame me," she whispered.

"Never."

She took two deep breaths and rubbed her hands over her upper arms. Errin shook her head in disbelief and fixed her eyes on his Adam's apple, which kept bobbing up and down.

He lifted her chin with his knuckles and repeated the words. "Never."

He traced the dimple in her cheek with his thumb as if it was distracting him from his big speech.

He gazed into her eyes and continued, "I want to see ye gallop through the fields, run around and experience every thrill life throws at ye. I want to stand beside ye, makin' sure I got ye back whenever ye need me. I'll never hold ye back, me darling filly. I want to make ye mine—yes. But never tame ye. Never."

"It's for ninety-nine percent certain I'll get the part. It's as good as promised to me. I'm going to Jersey, Bren. This has no future." She shook her head as she closed her eyes.

Austin

Brennan

16

Even though he realized it had to be like this, it still hurt like a mother. He was inflicting his heart pain by going through with this.

She was still set on moving back to Jersey to chase her dreams. But what was he to do? Stop this from happening tonight? Maybe she'd change her mind and stay. Maybe dancing there would suck and she'd come back on the first plane going to Texas. Maybe...

"I would never hold you back. Don't you know me by now? If..." he shook his head, "*When* you get that part in Jersey, I'll understand you must go and this is over. I promise I won't come up north crying and throwing myself at your feet. Okay?"

He pulled her satin underwear down until it circled her ankle when he picked her up by the back of her thighs. She instantly wrapped her arms around his neck, but she didn't respond to his words. He walked them over to his bedroom and slammed the door shut with the heel of his foot.

He laid her on top of his bed and leaned over her as he rested his under arms next to her head on the mattress.

His fingers found their way into her wavy, warm blonde hair that spread out over his pillow like poison ivy taking over his bed. She flung her good leg over his hip, causing just that sweet bit of friction between them.

"How's your ankle?" he whispered, nuzzling her neck. She gave an involuntary shiver and dug her nails into his upper back, arching her naked breasts against his chest.

He chuckled at her sudden inability to speak. His chuckling did the trick, because she placed her other foot on his back and growled, "Ankle is fine. Has been all week. Are you going to fuck me or not?"

He had to bear in mind she was talking with these brass balls because she wanted to screw with him. Not only in the flesh, but also screw with his head.

She wanted a hard fuck. Carnal. And most of all, impersonal. He understood where she was coming from. He'd hurt her feelings after they had sex the last time, by drawing the line in the sand and telling her to not go work for him or else he couldn't be with her anymore.

The way he went about things with Errin had been all kinds of wrong, and it had nagged him the past week. He'd watched Errin like a hawk, noticing her glances his way.

Her lingering eyes when he walked past her into the kitchen. The way she would scan the room to note his whereabouts. He wasn't some kind of crazy person. Their connection definitely wasn't a one-way-street.

This beautiful, mouthy and stubborn woman was as much invested in him as he was in her. He just had to break through her walls. Make her see how good they could be together. How he could elevate her and she him, just by being there for each other.

He leaned in and kissed her lips. The taste of lipstick, or rather the lack of taste, annoyed him as it reminded him of her dressing up for his cousin like some kind of Barbie doll. He pushed her legs down his back to the mattress and straddled her hips before sitting upright. She slumped, letting out a huge breath in the newfound space between them.

With his thumb, he smeared all make-up from her lips while she jerked her head vehemently away to stop him. Dark red smudges of lipstick now traced her dimpled cheeks. She swallowed twice but held her breath in anticipation for what was coming.

He took advantage of her wanting to wait and see his next move, by leaning in and kissing her again. But this time he kissed her more vigorously. The urgency to make her his was pouring from his kisses, licks and nibbles. She moaned while he kept on playing with her tongue.

He spread her legs with one of his and rubbed his muscular thigh against her pussy, making her grind into him in response. "Can't stand seein' ye with these fuckin' red lips. They look nothing like the lips that made me fall for ye," he whispered against her neck.

She gasped and flexed her fingers. Her entire body tensed at his admission, but her inner battle didn't discourage him. She gave her head a few deliberate, angry shakes in disbelief. "Stop. Don't even go there."

He'd expected this reaction. "Yes. Ye heard me, Lips. I've fallen for ye. These fuckin' luscious plump lips that never hold still, always talkin' 'bout shite, jokin' around and makin' me bat shit crazy."

"Okay. You're officially losing it, Brennan," she said as she closed her eyes and let out a forceful breath.

"Nah. Finally seein' what's been sittin' right in front of me these months. Don't care if I scare ye by admittin' it."

"You better stop this nonsense or let me go. Right now." She bristled and tried to get from under him. He held still above her and kissed away a lone tear that threatened to slip into her dimple.

Her breathing picked up when he placed his palm upon her

heart. It was pounding against her chest, almost trying as hard to escape as Errin tried to run from Brennan.

He wiped with his index finger under her eye to remove the proof he affected her. The first cracks in her armor showed and although he hated to make her cry, her emotions encouraged him.

His eyes went from her cheekbones dusted with freckles, to her dilated pupils, and he let her see inside his soul. He held her gaze to show he meant every single word. She couldn't distrust him with his heart pouring out his love for her.

"Yer perfect. Absolutely perfect for me."

"Bren..." Tears filled her eyes again.

"I'm gonna make ye mine, Lips. Tell me ye want to be mine."

She shook her head once but kept eyeing him intensively. Her wide eyes stared right at him, never blinking.

"I'm leaving, Bren. Stop talking like that. It can never work."

With his dark timbre he said, "Then say you'll be mine tonight. Let me have this one night." He held her eyes as he waited for her response.

"You're so intense. Too intense," she whispered.

"I'm honest. I'm not hiding my feelings for you," he said.

Her escaped sigh tickled his lips. She elevated her head the tiniest bit from his pillow and connected her lips with his. Her hands found his wavy black locks.

She didn't tug or pulled, she simply let her fingers part his strands and massage his scalp. Goose bumps traveled his skin, and he moaned against her mouth.

She opened up for him and leisurely met his tongue with hers. Their strokes were slow, sensual and without a sense of time.

Her perfect hard peaks scraped his chest, and he rubbed his pelvis against her. She hooked her leg around his back again and he rolled them halfway on the bed, never letting their lips part.

As they lay on their sides, he kissed the corner of her mouth, kissed her dimple, took her earlobe between his teeth for a loving tug and licked down to her collarbone. She let her hands wander over his muscular back and he shivered in her arms.

Her fingers went up again, and she scraped her red nails over the back of his neck. He couldn't help but growl at the sensation. Since she still had her leg hooked over his hip, he nudged his thigh higher between her legs to rub her core. The warm, slick sensation on his thigh almost did him in.

His hand caressed her skin, following the slight curve of her breast, down to her side. Some cute little jerks and a love bite on his bottom lip told him to remove his fingers from her ribs.

It reminded him of her tattoo he'd noticed when she'd send him that picture earlier. He kissed her collarbone and followed his hand down to her ribs with his lips.

I dance to the beat of my own drum

Her tattoo couldn't have suited her any better, and he smiled against her ribs before tracing the words with his tongue. She arched into him and he worked his way up again and rested his hand on the dimples of her lower back.

Her fingers stroked his beard on their way to his chin, keeping her hand in place before she nudged him in the most delicate way, testing if he would let her go on top.

He let his back fall to the mattress, and she immediately straddled him, raking her fingernails over his chin down to his neck. She took charge of the kiss, but kept their rhythm easy.

He enjoyed her taking the lead as she rocked her pussy back and forth against his dick, making it slick with her juices.

He would stop her before he couldn't hold back long enough to get a condom, but first he would enjoy how she was making herself come by pushing herself against him.

He held still at the delicious sight of her perfect handful of tits, as they swayed the tiniest bit by her movements. She moaned while fisting his dick. *Oh fuck, she was going to put him in?*

"Errin…" he warned. She halted all movement, and he groaned, "I want to be inside ye so bad right now. Let me grab a condom."

She responded by sliding down his body and kissing him along her way. Her swirling tongue plagued his nipple, followed by another swirl lower and lower, halting above his belly button.

She studied him with the hottest grin on her face and then scooted to the foot of the bed, placing her knees together between his thighs and her hands next to his hips.

She licked his shaft from the base to the top, making his hard dick jerk up from his abdomen. By taking his erection into her mouth, she drove him crazy with that same fuckin' swirling tongue going round and over the crown. Bolts of pleasure shot straight to his core. Her hands were still not into the game, making him imagine how it would feel if they were pumping his dick.

His breathing picked up when her hand first massaged his balls but suddenly went lower. Her index finger massaged him there, the spot that made him lose his vision as bright spots came before his eyes. She titillated his perineum, and he shouted, "Fuck! Errin gonna come…."

He spurted his cum into her fiery mouth and she swallowed around him, spurring his orgasm along, making him come like no other had. He opened his eyes, and she was still licking him, kissing his dick like she couldn't get enough of it, of all of him. His cock jerked at the sight before him, and she giggled.

A smile crept over his face and he flipped them around so she sat squarely on his face, his beard scratching her lean thighs as he moved his head to get a better position to pleasure her. Her knees dented his pillow beside his ears, and her hands gripped the wall for balance.

He caressed her perky ass, kneading her warm flesh. He nuzzled her pussy, tickling her clit. She moved against him, matching his rhythm as he tongued her.

"Oh, Bren. Yes... right... there..." she moaned, her voice pained.

He licked her cream like she did his. Lapping everything up and letting her juices coat his face. She tasted sweet and salty and everything in between. He couldn't get enough of her.

He traced his index finger between her folds for lubricant and placed the finger in the crack of her arse, letting it trace her spot right there. He caressed the entry, teasing her by doing so.

"Aaaah do it. Yes... mmm put it in," she pined.

He breached the tight ring of muscle with his finger while he kept on assaulting her pussy with his tongue. She quivered on his face when he fucked her arse with his finger. He took her throbbing clit between his teeth and gave a gentle tug. Her need for more friction led her to ride his face; rock her pussy back and forth.

The most feral moan escaped her throat as she came. Her lower back was hot and slick with sweat under his hand and her thighs clamped his ears as she rode out her orgasm. When her movements finally stilled, he withdrew his finger. She moaned a little softer this time around at the loss of this pressure inside of her.

She scooted lower beside him and nestled herself under his arm. He placed his hand on her butt, caging her in and pulling her close to his side. She flung her leg over him, resting her knee rather close to his now soft cock.

He kissed the top of her head, probably making it all sticky with her own cum by doing so. He chuckled, and she tilted her head back to meet his eyes.

"What?" she gave him the sweetest little smile while biting her bottom lip, and his heart skipped a beat.

"Makin' your hair all sticky..." he said as he waggled his brows.

"Don't give a fuck," she said and climbed his upper body to give his lips a messy and sticky kiss. He groaned against her lips before opening and kissing her back.

"Love your dirty mouth," he said.

She giggled and Errin, being Errin, upped it by saying, "Fuck, you eat me so good. I get wet thinking about you licking me."

"Yer better stop right there, Lips," he warned as he grabbed a handful of her arse. She would be the death of him, already getting him hard again.

She smiled like she was ignorant of why he got so agitated.

"What? It's true."

She shrugged and laid her head in the crook of his neck. He smiled, as she didn't move a muscle to go clean herself in the bathroom.

He lay perfectly happy with her in his arms, as she didn't even try to tell him one of her stupid jokes.

He sure as hell wouldn't bring any ideas into her head by addressing it. He let out a big breath and held her even closer.

She woke up in his bed and sure enough; the sound of the shower running in his attached bathroom disappointed her.

Disappointed, because she'd rather lay all sticky and smelly against his hot body for a few moments longer. *What was wrong with me?*

She glanced around his room like she had on the night of her birthday celebration. This time completely relaxed and satisfied. She jumped when Brennan entered the bedroom.

He had little room to move around his king-size bed as he walked over to his closet. His unruly wet black hair stood out on all sides of his head and his short trimmed beard glinted from some kind of lotion.

The scent of sandalwood wafted into the room and she took a deep breath to fill her lungs with his smell.

He chuckled at her antics while dropping his towel and said, "Ah, you finally awake, eh?"

He turned his naked backside to her to open his closet. Some stray water droplets slid down his spine, gliding over his naked white firm cheeks, showing the exact measurement of the swim shorts he wore during the summer.

She licked her lips and cleared her throat before remembering his words.

"*Finally?*"

"Yeah. I already did my workout in the living room. Figured I should let you sleep in."

She sat up in bed and said, "You could've woken me up, Bren."

He glanced over his shoulder and raised his brow. "Not really a morning person, eh?"

She huffed a breath, and he smirked like he couldn't hold his laughter. As he hummed to himself while picking out clothes, she crossed her arms and blew a stray strand of hair from her face.

This was all too much. He was acting like they were in a relationship, standing all-naked before her, talking about letting her sleep in. Should she set him straight?

His black boxer briefs showed under his still open blue faded jeans and as her eyes found his, he was smiling down at her. She sure was tempted to go all Evil Errin on his ass, cussing him out for not listening to her. She told him they would fuck one last time and that would be it.

Argh, last night he'd said he was falling for her! Shit. And after he'd said so, she had sex with him, anyway. She should put some distance between them. Maybe quit working at the pub all together. But what if the audition ended up like the rest of them lately had?

She swallowed back the emotions threatening to clog her throat. She needed to get away from him for a moment. He would have her crying like nobody's business if he said something sweet to her. Ugh.

She stood from the bed and walked into the bathroom. After doing her business, she picked a toothbrush from under the sink. She opened the packaging and smeared a generous amount of toothpaste on the blue brush.

She looked up into the mirror, and snorted when her reflection equaled a fucked up clown with red smudges surrounding her lips, even coloring her cheeks.

He'd detested her make-up. Ha! And he really didn't like her drinking with his cousin. She snickered and leaned down to spit residue toothpaste into the sink.

She was still butt naked, so she walked into his shower stall and turned on the shower. After a few moments beneath the stream of warm water, she started washing her hair with his shampoo. The typical Brennan scent enveloped her hair and body like a warm blanket. She jumped from a knock on the bathroom door.

"I'll make us some breakfast. What would you like?" he asked behind the door.

"I'll have whatever you're having, thanks," she said before she stuck her bottom lip under the spray, letting the stream fall from both sides of her mouth, and coming together over her chin.

Him making breakfast for her almost gave her a panic attack. She had to have 'the talk' with him. Maybe over breakfast.

She sighed and washed her body once more. Tears threatened to fall and stung her eyes. She tilted her head back under the spray and let the water wash away the evidence of her emotions.

"Geez. Such a cry-baby," she whispered. "Grow some balls, Errin. Tell him where you stand. Before it gets too hard to leave him."

She turned off the faucet and picked up the towel from the counter that hadn't been there when she'd entered the shower stall. Huh. He sure had some mad ninja skills. She grinned.

After towel drying her hair and braiding it in her signature messy style, she entered the bedroom and picked up his dark blue T-shirt he'd lain out for her at the foot of the bed. She picked up the T and smelled it. *Mmm, Brennan.*

She entered the open-plan kitchen and walked over with determined steps to this sexy man, sitting at the table, just about to take a bite from his partially burnt toast. He held it still mid air to his mouth and studied her as she climbed onto his lap, straddling his strong thighs.

Her palms covered his beard, and she leaned in to give him a sweet kiss on his full lips. She held his gaze. "Just so we're clear. This was great and all—"

"Hmmm. Just great, eh?" he said while grabbing a stronger hold of her bum.

"Yeah. Wasn't it?" she shrugged.

"It was more than great, Lips. And because I realize I've spooked you last night with what I said, I won't repeat my words. I'll tell you this, however; I never expected an eleven year younger filly—"

She held her fingers against his lips. His eyes grew wide before he narrowed them.

"Just... enjoy this. Stop talking about whatever feelings you think you have."

He swatted her butt as to motion for her to stop her line of thinking.

"It's true. It's a very good possibility I'll be leaving for good. You said you wouldn't get in between me and dancing." She raised a brow and held his eyes.

He swallowed and nodded once.

"Okay then. Let's eat."

She climbed from his lap after giving him one last peck and sat next to him at the kitchen table.

"So, what are we having?" she said with clasped hands against her chin, glancing around the full table, growing more and more enthusiastic by so much mouthwatering smelling food.

He cleared his throat and blinked once before shaking his head.

"Uhm, yeah. I figured one couldn't go wrong with a simple toast and fried eggs and bacon, but just in case, I've also made a bowl with some fruit for you. I hope you like bananas, apples, and blueberries? That shit is good for you."

She smiled at his last statement. Who knew this burly, older man could be so soft and sweet? He was just like a stuffed animal. From the outside, he was a wild beast, but he was all squishy and soft on the inside. She chuckled and shook her head.

"What?" he said with a smile in his voice.

"Nothing, just..." She shrugged. "I like you." She said before she could stop herself. She trained her eyes on her plate. As she smeared butter on her toast she said, "But I'm still going to Jersey."

He hummed but said nothing back. So she risked a glance next to her and directly met his blazing eyes. She shot from her chair. She opened the fridge and asked, "Do you want some orange juice?"

He huffed a breath and said, "Yeah. That would be great."

She scanned the fridge from top to bottom, but came up empty. "You're outta luck, there's none left."

When she closed the fridge and walked back to the table, she halted mid-step when he was in the middle of pouring a second glass of OJ with a shit-eating grin.

"What the fuck?" she spat at him.

"Well, it stood right in front of you, Lips. But I guess you—" he started. But she would not stand for him calling her out on running from him after admitting she liked him.

"Ah, shut yer handsome face. I just woke up. Give a girl a break, will ye?" she said as she plopped down next to a smiling Brennan.

"Talkin' like a true Irish lass. Pops would be so proud of ye." He laughed.

Thankfully, he was smiling again. She didn't want to risk having a Broody Brennan at this table and held her tongue while she ate her toast.

"Since we're both free today..." he said while picking up a slice of apple, "Maybe we could do something together?"

He studied her reaction as he put the whole slice in between his juicy lips. Her thighs clenched at the memory of these same lips pleasuring her last night.

Just before she wanted to tell him no, he held up his hand and said, "Just as friends... with benefits. Does that work for you?"

"Hmmm. Erm, yeah. I guess we can hang," she said, still mesmerized by his lips and his throat, ultimately swallowing the slice down.

She took the last bite of her toast and glared at him when he snickered. "Hang?"

She sat up straight and picked up her orange juice. "Yeah, old man. Hang. Geez."

She took a hefty gulp to cool down from his smiling face. My God, he was even more handsome with that carefree look on his face. That she probably had something to do with that, gave her a warm feeling inside. He also was making her hot—very hot. She downed the last drop from her juice and stood from her chair to clear the table.

"No, please let me," he said as he stood and reached over the table to get her plate. They were now both holding her plate, and she was the first to tug it in her direction, but stubborn Brennan wouldn't let go.

"Bren. Please, let me. You've cooked us breakfast. Least I can do is clear the table." A vision of her swooping all dishes from the table to the ground to clear the table and letting him eat her out on top of it entered her mind and in that moment, Brennan closed the distance between them.

"I need you again."

He spoke in a dark, low rumble and took the plate from her hands with a firm tug. She jumped from her spot and grabbed his shoulders for leverage. She hooked her legs around his hips and giggled as the plate smashed against the kitchen tiles.

He laughed along with her and grabbed the back of her head before he gave her a hard, demanding kiss, full of energy. She crossed her ankles behind his back and let her fingers play with his longer hair on top of his head. He walked them over to his couch, but suddenly turned around and changed course.

Before she could ask, he already said, "Condoms. Going to fuck ye this time." He groaned as she licked behind his ear before whispering, "Finally."

"I don't think I can do this."

"Sure you can, Lips," Brennan said.

Errin looked over her shoulder to Brennan, who stood a few feet behind her. She shook her head with wide eyes. "No. I really—like *really* think I can't do this."

Her hands on the side of the black stallion followed the horse as it took a tugging step forward, causing Errin to side-step too. "See. The horse agrees. He wants me to scram too." She waved her arms in the air, making the horse stamp his foot.

Brennan took a few pensive steps toward Errin, careful not to spook the beautiful animal. He laid his hand on top of Errin's tense shoulder and leaned in to whisper in her ear. "Relax, baby girl. If you'll relax, the horse will too."

She let her shoulders fall in defeat. "I'm an open book Bren, you know that. I can't pretend I'm happy to be here. He's so big. So...unpredictable. I don't like it."

Brennan engulfed her slight frame with his and tentatively laid his large hand on top of the warm horse's coat. The animal raised its head and neck, positioning one ear forward and one ear back. But after a few pets of Brennan, the horse loosened his lower lip and relaxed.

"You still got it, Bren," Fianna said as she walked up to them.

She gave the stallion's nose a few loving strokes, and the animal nickered in greeting.

"Good. That's right. Everything's fine." Fianna leaned in and spoke against the horse's neck while petting his coat. At these stables, Fianna let her prickly guard down.

He watched the fiery redhead in riding gear as she kept whispering against the horse's neck. Did his brother Ronan fell for this softer side of her? Or was it Fianna's fierceness she normally showed whenever she'd opened her mouth?

"Do you come here often, Bren?" Errin asked. She looked from Brennan over to Fianna and back as she crossed her arms in front of her dark blue shirt.

He shrugged. "It's my aunt's farm, so every now and then. But when Ro still came around here, I'd tag along more often."

"Ronan rides?" Errin asked in a high-pitched voice. The horse neighed, and Errin jumped. Brennan took Errin by her shoulders and directed her a few steps back.

The tied horse stood in his open stable, but Brennan felt safer now she was out of reach from the animal. He knew Fianna could handle the horse, but he wasn't risking it around Errin.

"Pssht. Can you picture that enormous lump of arrogance on a horse?" Fianna sneered.

Yep. His youngest brother is still a hot topic. Even though it had been over for quite some time now—years even, both Ro and Fianna had trouble to let go of the hurt.

Their childish bickering was annoying and often awkward for all innocent bystanders.

"Fi," Brennan said as he narrowed his eyes at her.

"Yeah, yeah. Okay." Fianna held up her hand.

"For your information, Errin... The first time Ro and I dated, he was still a boy and... well, less apelike and definitely less obnoxious."

"Fi…"

"Well, it's true. Ever since he's gone wild on fighting at those MMA things and screwing everything that's female with a still beating heart, he's grown into…" she pulled her dainty shoulders and elbows and motioned her arms wide from her waist like a stereotype bodybuilder, "an arrogant, obnoxious, idiot gorilla."

Errin shook her head, giggling as Fi mimicked Ronan. Brennan grabbed Errin's hand in his and squeezed. She looked up to him, smiling, and he sucked in a breath. Showing Errin around his family's farm where Fianna worked with the horses had been exactly what they needed today.

When he was younger, he'd spent lots of weekends with his brothers and some Ryan sisters at the farm his aunt Shauni and her husband Roger ran.

His cousin Emmy experimented with own-farmed products from the fields while growing up. Her mother Shauni never cooked as good as Emmy, and her entire family applauded Emmy when she suggested taking over the cooking for the farmhands and their family.

After screwing each other's brains out this morning, he'd figured he should take Errin outside to get her away from every flat surface he could fuck her on. And by doing so, he wanted to show her another side of Texas, just a few miles outside of Austin.

They'd spent the afternoon petting kittens, looking at some pigs rolling around in mud and walking around in the open air without a care in the world. He was deluding himself.

But fuck if he would not take all of her time she had left in Austin. She'd said she was flying to Jersey during Lucky's renovation and leaving this Wednesday. It gave them three more days together.

He would make most of it. In other words, leave this horse-shit smelling stable to take her home with him.

"Okay. We're heading back. Thanks again for showing us around, Fi."

"No problem. See you later, Errin," Fianna said as she turned to Errin.

"Yeah, thanks Fianna for giving me a tour. Are you still coming on Tuesday? We can have a drink together before I leave," Errin said.

"Wouldn't miss it. It's just us girl's right?" Fi said before she picked up a bucket with water.

"We're joining you girls later at Thomas Tavern. I'm not missing out on Errin's last night in Austin," Brennan said while stroking the apple of Errin's cheek.

"We as in the Mills testosterone brigade?" Fianna said before she pursed her lips.

"Ha! I'm so glad my last name is Moore."

Brennan turned around to the voice of his cousin Ryan, Emmy's brother. The poor guy had five younger sisters.

Not that he would ever ridicule him or anything; the big fucker could take him out cold with a single shot. Those bales of hay were natural deadlifts, making him even stronger than his MMA fighting brother.

"Hey, Ry. How's it going, Cuz?" He grabbed Ryan's hand and tugged him in a one-armed man hug. Ryan slapped his back, and Brennan did his best to hide his grimace.

His cousin didn't throw his force around to establish dominance. He often was unaware of his own strength when he slung his big guns around. Brennan was sure Ryan was even holding back.

"All good. I'd like you to meet Errin. She's... erm, she—" Before he could make a bigger arse of himself, Errin stepped up with her hand stretched out in front of her.

"Hi, Ryan. You're Emmy's brother, right? Hi. I'm Errin. I work with your sister at Lucky." They shook hands and Brennan let go of the breath he was holding.

"*You're* Errin?" Ryan asked with a smirk as he took the time to trail his brown eyes over Errin's tight fitted jeans, up to her small waist, over her perky breasts beneath Brennan's borrowed T-shirt and finally resting his eyes on her face. This was the second cousin he wanted to knock the fuck out for blatantly eyeing Errin.

Errin placed her fisted hands on top of her hips and jutted her chin toward Ryan who now had his eyebrows raised so high, they reached the black locks of hair that fell over his forehead.

"Why don't you believe I'm Errin?" Errin said as she cocked her head. Fianna snickered while scooping up some horseshit with a shovel. "Here we go..." Fianna singsonged before dumping a pile of manure into a wheelbarrow.

Ryan held up his hand and said, "Ah, sorry. Don't mean to offend you. It's just... well, let's say at first glance, you look nothing like the spitfire my sister described you as."

Brennan took a step closer to Errin's back and held her small hips in his hands. She glanced over her shoulder at Brennan and grinned as she said, "Hmm. Okay. I get that a lot."

Ryan looked over Errin's head at Brennan and with one shared look between cousins, Brennan told Ryan to back off from his girl. Ryan gave him a curt nod and said, "So, Errin. How d'ya like our farm?"

"I love it! Can't wait to come back sometime."

"You do that, Spitfire. You do that," Ryan said as he laughed at his cousin's narrowed eyes.

Suddenly, Errin broke in a fit of laughter and said, "Wait? Is your dad's name really Roger?" Ryan let out a fake groan, but he smiled at Errin. "Yeah, yeah. We've heard the jokes all before, Spitfire."

"So, is it true then?" Errin said. Brennan counted till three in his head, as he was sure she was aiming for a joke about his uncle's name he'd never heard before. Back in the days, his aunt Shauni liked to boost about her farmer husband being sexier than his namesake, the former James Bond actor.

Ryan grinned as he signaled with his hands and said, "Okay. Give it to me. I bet I've heard it already…"

"Just wondering if your dad shook while making you and stirred while making your four sisters?"

Brennan busted out in laughter along with Fi. Ryan's eyed grew wide before he joined them. "Okay, okay. I'm going to tell Roger Moore this joke tonight at the dinner table. You've got me there, Spitfire."

"You do that, Ryan Moore," Errin said on a wink.

Brennan took Errin's hand and tugged her with him as he took the first steps out of the stables. He didn't care about being rude. He said goodbye over his shoulder and Errin snickered. "Geez, the Mills testosterone brigade is on full force today."

As he rode his truck from the farmland, she broke their moment of silence. "Can I ask you something?"

"Sure. What's up?"

He glanced over at Errin, sitting in her light blue jeans they'd picked up at her place, and his dark blue shirt she'd lend this morning.

She did that tying thing chicks did whenever their shirt was too big. It made his shirt bunch up in a knot above her belly button ring. It was making him crazy. Thinking of his cousin Ryan seeing her piercing made him see red.

"What's your story?"

His gaze went from her piercing to her eyes and he swiftly turned his head toward the road ahead. "What do you mean, Lips? That's a pretty vague question."

"Like I said. What's your story? Why are you the way you are?"

He'd figured he was rather used to Errin's bluntness and directness by now. But she still surprised him. "I'm not sure I want to get into all of that."

"Why?"

He turned left and followed the road once more. "Lips. Not everyone wants to talk about everything. Or all the time, for that matter," he said the last words under his breath as his knuckles turned white on the steering wheel. She snickered while he sighed. She wasn't easily deterred and took his mutters in stride.

"Okay. Since we have half an hour to kill, I'll tell you a bit about what formed me," he said.

Errin turned her body toward him. She eyed him closely, and he shifted in his seat. Fuck. Was he really going to tell her what for shit show their past had been after his mom had died? It was not like Brennan to tell someone his life story. But this was Errin.

"My mom died when I was fourteen. Let's say, my dad couldn't handle all the responsibilities. And that's putting it mildly. He was out working in Lucky or sleeping in late because of the late shifts. He would often also stay over at the apartment above Lucky, my apartment now, and whenever that was the case, we wouldn't see him for several days in a row.

"And whenever he *would* turn up at the house, he acted like the carefree fun dad, messing up with the schedules I'd set for the boys and interfering with the chores they had to do around the house. Things escalated quickly between him and me."

"That's—"

"Yeah, well, the only thing I'm thankful for is that Sean Jr. made me the rock that all my brothers could depend on. I'll never regret setting my own hopes and dreams aside to be there for them."

After a few beats, she asked, "What were your hopes and dreams?"

He shook his head and gave a smile that didn't reach his eyes. "I wanted to be a pilot."

"Oh, you'd make such a handsome pilot. I'd join your mile high club in a heartbeat." She placed her hand on his thigh, making him look over at the heat in her eyes.

"I'd do you a mile high, a mile low. Fuck, I'd do you anywhere," he said.

Her signature loud laugh filled the cabin. "I'll bet. You're such a horndog."

"Pfft. It takes two to tango. I'm surprised you didn't know, seeing you're a dancer."

The moment the words came out, he regretted them. It reminded them both of the expiration date of their arrangement. The friends with benefits thing was a disaster waiting to happen. He glanced once more over his shoulder.

Errin gazed out of the window. What he wouldn't give to have a peak inside that magnificent mind of her right now.

"Why did you turn so cold after... after the first time we..." she said.

"When we fucked for the first time?" he raised a brow. It was unlike Errin to not just spit it out. It must still strike a nerve with her, thinking about that day. Shit.

"I didn't want to be like my dad, baby girl. He fucked everything with a skirt at Lucky. It didn't matter if they were customers or even young women who worked for him. He had absolutely no self-control. I promised myself, after walking in on him once, that I would never—*ever*, turn out like Sean Jr."

She squeezed his thigh, giving him some kind of reassurance. He took a deep breath and said, "I was wrong that day we argued, Errin. The moment we got together, I felt in my gut it meant so much more than I could comprehend at the time. But I let my own damn rules come between us. I hurt you that day, saying we couldn't be together if you'd work for me. I'm sorry, baby girl."

She bit her lip and gave him her smile. The smile that made his heart skip a few beats. "Please say something," he said.

"I needed to hear this, Bren. Thank you," she whispered in an unlike Errin manner.

"I'm sorry, I guess being brought up in an all male household didn't teach me much manners. I should've said I was sorry a long time ago."

"Hmmm, you're right. I think I should teach you some manners, Bren."

"Do you have something in mind?" He stopped his truck in front of a red light and looked over at Errin. The light catching her light blue eyes drew him in, making them sparkle even more with mischief.

"Sure. I have my ways to punish you, all right." She winked, and her smile deepened the dimple in her cheeks. He traced a dimple with his thumb and moved over to her plump pink lips.

She opened and sucked his thumb in, warming it with her wet tongue. His dick grew against his zipper. "You're making me hard, Lips."

"Hmmm-mmm." She licked once more and sucked. Her cheeks hollowed, and he imagined how she would lick him there. His painful, raging hard on was weeping at her touch.

She let his thumb go with a plop and said, "Green."

"What?"

A horn sounded behind his truck, bringing him out of his daze.

"Shit. Can't wait till you punish me some more, Lips." He glanced at the time on his dashboard. "ETA is ten minutes."

She laughed and said, "Such a pilot thing to say. Aren't you going to comment on the weather on the ground? How we got lucky with the speed of wind that would bring us a few minutes ahead of schedule?" she mocked.

He snorted. "Yeah, yeah. Maybe I should go with you on the plane on Wednesday. Get us in the mile high club."

"Bren..."

"Just joking." He playfully nudged her knee with his knuckles, but in the pit of his stomach the knot grew tighter.

Austin

Errin
19

"So, Errin, I heard from my brother you've got some mad jokes." Aiden grinned while he rammed his sledge-hammer once more against the poor old bar that stood on its last legs after Aiden's profuse power plays.

She cleared her throat after ogling his tight faded blue jeans and sturdy arms peeping from under a black T-shirt with the Mills Construction logo on the back.

Next to her, Brennan rolled his eyes but surprisingly enough, held his tongue.

"I would gladly tell you a construction joke, but I'm still working on it," she said before winking at the very hot younger brother of Keenan, who eyed her over his shoulder. The Mills men laughed at her joke, and Keenan shook his head. "Told ya."

Damn. The Mills DNA made her mouth water. Like all Mills boys, Aiden was well above six feet tall and he had the same strong build. Perhaps even more muscular because of his profession as a builder.

His dark brown hair stood in a faux mohawk and his thick brown beard made him look like his cousin Ronan. But his twinkling light green eyes matched Brennan's.

She glanced up at Brennan and couldn't help but stand on her tiptoes and nibble his bottom lip. He was so beautiful, even now with a big scowl on his face. She giggled against his protruded lip.

They were inseparable these last few days, and she sure wasn't homesick anymore. Conner had called her yesterday, and the moment he'd talked about Jersey, panic sat in. She actually considered Lucky and now even Brennan her home.

The only thing pushing her to the auditions was her promise to herself. She was going on a plane tomorrow to go see for one last time if she could make it as a dancer. It had been her hope and dream she'd be a part of a big production. Dancing had always been her life. A few days filled with hot sex shouldn't deter her from her goals. Right?

"I'm going to see if I can help Emmy," she said.

Brennan held her close against him and kissed her again. With one hand at the back of her head, he deepened their kiss. His big calloused hand roamed her butt and their body heat made her pantomiming fanning herself as she broke the kiss. If this was for show, for his cousins to warn them off of her, she didn't know nor cared.

"Mmm. I hope the freezer still works. Goin' to sit my ass down there for a while to cool off. If you need me, you'll know where to find me."

Brennan gave her a lopsided grin and tapped her butt twice. The Mills cousins had their eyes on her as she walked past them, but she gave them no further attention.

To ogle them from a safe distance was one thing, but flirting with these guys was something that wouldn't go over so well with Brennan. And she understood where he was coming from. She always figured she didn't have an insecure bone in her body, but somehow being with this attractive older man made her seeing green.

It was a good thing Lucky was closed for a few weeks so she didn't have to work alongside her co-worker Tori for a while.

Tori's heated stares at Brennan rubbed her the wrong way now he was off the market. Okay, kind of off the market.

A female co-worker who didn't annoy her was busy instructing her uncle Niall about the layout of the new kitchen. Emmy and Niall hunched over a rolled out plan over the stainless steel worktable.

"The sink is now placed next to the griddle grills, but I think the first thing we need to do is place a commercial grill on that side…" Emmy waved to her far left. "And the new stainless steel counters there." Emmy nodded to her right. "And the dishwasher over there."

Niall Mills was busy penning everything down and hummed along. He glanced over at Errin as she joined them. "You're Brennan's girl, right?" He stuck out his hand and his gray eyes smiled as they shook hands.

"Well, that's a long story. But I think I'm the one and only—for now." She tried to joke.

Niall snorted and said, "Nah. My nephew ain't like that, lass. He ain't nothing like my brother."

Emmy cleared her throat, the conversation making her uncomfortable. Niall side-eyed his niece from under his thick, dark eyebrows—the only facial hair left that hadn't turned gray and grinned.

"You know I'm not lying. Sean Jr.—" he started, but the man himself interrupted him by walking into the kitchen.

"Can't believe how ya'll are tearin' this place down. My life's work…" Sean Jr. waved his hands around and continued. "Our dad's life's work…."

"Ah, stop it. You've had your time and now you've got to let the youngsters take over. Simple as that. Let your boy do what's necessary and don't give him any headaches 'bout it."

"You've never liked Lucky," Sean Jr. said. "Showed no interest in our family's pub. I can't believe he's letting you wreck this place. It must give you some sick rush to knock everything down."

Niall laid his pencil down and puffed out his chest. Emmy placed her hand on top of her uncle's but Niall didn't acknowledge her touch.

"It wasn't Lucky that I was tryin' to avoid, brother. It was you. But I guess you'd been too busy stickin' yer head between random women's legs to realize what really was going on."

Errin watched the two brothers ping-ponged their retorts with the stainless work counter as the ping-pong table between them. Apparently, Brennan wasn't the only one who had a problem with Sean Jr.

Sometimes, Errin wondered if her jokes were a nervous tic, but she bit her lip to not throw in another joke to stop these brothers from bickering. She was this close to blurt something, but she also wanted to understand the beef between them.

"Always been the jealous little brother." Sean Jr. snorted.

"Nah, I'm sorry that's not it." Niall scoffed and leaned over the worktable. "But truthfully? I looked up to you when Edith was still alive. Seein' what you had with her and the boys was—"

Sean Jr. leaned in from his side of the table and bristled. "Don't. You. Mention. Her. Name."

Niall shrugged. "You had it all. And after Edith died, you fucked it all up."

Sean Jr. slammed both fists on top of the worktable, denting the stainless steel and roared, "Try me. Ye say her name one more time and I swear I'll kick yer arse."

"What do you call a singing kitchen utensil?" Errin spat from her side of the kitchen.

All three heads whipped in her direction, almost if they had forgotten all about her standing there.

"Nobody? Emmy?" she said.

Emmy furrowed her brows and threw a look her way as if she needed to have her head examined.

Sean Jr. cleared his throat. "Now is not the time, sweet girl."

Errin walked over to the two former raging bulls, now standing in a state of annoyance or rather confusion. She grinned because Sean Jr.'s dismissal didn't discourage her—well, not exactly.

She gave it her all as she threw her hands out in the air and sang from the top of her lungs, "A spatu-laaaaaaah."

"Christ. She really Brennan's girl?" Niall asked his brother with a quirked brow.

Sean Jr. shook his head while chuckling. "Yes. Can you imagine her telling her jokes to Bren?"

Niall bellowed a laugh and grabbed a hold of his strong abdomen. Keenan and Aiden's dad obviously still kept in shape by doing hard labor as a construction worker.

Looks wise, he resembled Keenan, only twenty years their senior with a short trimmed gray beard and wavy slight gray hair on top. Niall wiped a tear from under his eye. "That I've got to see."

Sean Jr. laughed along with his brother and grabbed Errin's shoulder and tugged her into his side. He kissed the top of her hair. "A sight to behold, I swear. I've never seen me boy happier. Sorry for being short with you, dear lass."

She let his remark slide about her being together with Brennan. She nodded and shot a glance at Niall, who cocked his head and waited for what was to come.

But she figured her work was done here since it had broken the tension and the two brothers had even laughed together. At her expense, but that didn't matter to Errin. She smiled at Niall and said, "You want another joke, eh? I see it in your eyes."

He laughed and shook his head. "Priceless. I've heard about you. My boy Keenan speaks real highly of you."

Sean Jr.'s hand tensed on her shoulder, just for a second, but she'd felt it, anyway. She laughed. "Ah, that's nice of him. He's a great guy. If I had a single sister, I would definitely send her his way, but alas..."

Niall snickered and said, "So, Brennan it is?"

She nodded and without missing a beat said, "Yep."

"Damn, Dad. You never quit pimping me out, eh?" Keenan spoke behind her back. "Although this time, I can't argue with you."

She turned her head to look over her shoulder at Keenan who winked at her, before Brennan shoulder checked him on his way to Errin. Errin looked over at Emmy, who snorted and rolled her eyes at her cousins.

"Errin, care to ditch all the testosterone for a while?" Emmy asked. "My uncle and I are done with the plans so I can go shop for some extra kitchen stuff. Maybe find some new... spatu-laaaahs," she singsonged. Not as loud as Errin—but still.

"Damn. It's contagious," Niall joked as he jabbed Emmy in the ribs with his elbow. Emmy giggled and said to Errin, "So, let's get out of here."

"Sure, let me grab my stuff. I'll see you at the back door, okay?"

"Okay," Emmy said.

Before she could walk out of the kitchen, Brennan held her to his chest and hugged her tight. "After today, we're never having karaoke night at Lucky," Brennan said with a smile in his voice.

She glanced up at him and grinned, "Ah, you heard me?"

"Yeah," he said. "Glad we already packed all the glassware away."

She poked his ribs with her index finger before he took her hand and guided it from his body.

"Mmm. That's a shame. I love karaoke. But never mind. I can

always do some coyote ugly and lip-synch. You've noticed I have the moves...." She waggled her eyebrows.

Some snorts and snickers surrounded them, but Brennan raised his brows in question. "Coyote ugly?"

"Geez. How old are you, exactly?"

"Irish fire, I'll tell ye," Pops said from the kitchen doorway.

Brennan kissed her lips and said, "Don't I know it."

After grabbing her purse from Brennan's apartment, Errin walked out the back door and over to Emmy, who already had her car running.

The green paint from her old Honda van peeled off at several spots, and when Errin tried to open the dented door, it got stuck.

"Sorry, my baby is twelve years old, but still rides like a dream," Emmy said while pushing the door open from the inside, as she hung over the passenger's side.

"Whoa, you sure we're safe in this thing? Does it even have seatbelts?" Errin said.

"This *thing*? My Hondy is the best," Emmy said while patting the steering wheel.

The holes and stains in the worn seat made Errin weary, but what scrunched her nose was the smell coming from the trash stashed in the door, on the floor of the car and between the seats.

"What the hell is this, Emm? How can this be your car when Lucky's kitchen is always so sparkling clean it hurts my eyes?"

Emmy giggled and shrugged. "Are you coming or what? Geez..."

Errin smiled and sat down after swiping the crumpled brown drive thru bags down to the floor. She made room for her jean-clad legs and white sneakers by kicking it to the side.

She glanced over at Emmy, who had turned on her car radio, filling the silence with some old R&B tunes. There were no USB ports, no navigation, no nothing. Just a girl with an old dirty car and a radio.

Errin rather liked this side of Emmy. "So, what's there to know about Emmy?" she started.

Emmy laughed and said, "Always so direct. I knew it was coming."

Errin sat back in her seat and shifted when a straw poked her back. She snatched the thing and pointed it at Emmy. "So shoot."

Emmy swallowed a few times before she shot a glance at Errin. "Okay. We're friends, but I don't think I'm ready to tell you my life story just yet. Sorry. No offence, but... yeah." She shrugged a shoulder and turned the car into a street that Errin didn't recognize. But that wasn't uncommon, as she'd only lived in Austin for a few months.

"Okay. I respect that. It's not like I'm an open book," Errin said.

Emmy snorted. "I wouldn't be so sure about that. You're pretty easy to read."

Errin shifted her seat to turn her body to Emmy and after folding her arms she said, "Ha. Try me."

"Okay. You're a dancer by heart. You're passionate about expressing yourself. I guess not only by talking all the time but also by your dancing. You have an open mind, because I know I can come off bitchy and you still made the effort to befriend me." Emmy stopped the car for a red light and locked eyes with Errin.

"Whenever people get emotional, you don't like it. You rather tell a stupid joke than dealing with whichever emotion you've got boiling inside. I'm still not sure if that's something that's got to do with a trauma or if you just work that way."

"No trauma. I just can't stand tension or seeing people cry, I want to cheer them up and make things better. Dunno." Errin let her words trail and said, "Green."

"What?"

"The light. It's green." Errin laughed. "You drive just like Brennan. He doesn't watch the lights turn either."

"That brings me to my cousin. You're scared to admit you're questioning the whole going back up north thing. What you've got with Bren is special. You don't want to leave him, but you don't want to go back on your dreams or goals or what the fuck ever."

"Well, maybe I am an open book after all," Errin said and added on a disappointed note, "Thought I was a lot more mysterious, damn."

Emmy laughed. "We can't have it all."

Errin stuck her tongue out to Emmy and laughed.

"Okay, then start with something easy. Ah! I know! I've met your brother Ryan the other day. Hotness overload." Errin fanned herself, and Emmy rolled her eyes.

"Please. Never repeat that to his face. My brother's got a big enough head as it is," she said.

"Ooh, I love me a good big head on top of a hard long—" Errin crooned, but Emmy interrupted her by honking her horn in an annoyingly long wail.

"Shut up, Errin. Those words in combination of my brother..." Emmy fake shuddered and Errin busted out laughing.

"Was just messing with you, Emm. Geez." She smiled over at Emmy, who tried to hide her smile by looking over her shoulder to switch lanes.

The car behind them honked several times. "Jerk," Emmy muttered. "Definitely compensating something with that prissy sports car."

Errin laughed and looked over the back of her seat at the

angry middle-aged man with a comb over. He flipped Errin the bird, and she couldn't help but smile.

"Classic. Now he's giving me the finger. Like, dude... I'm not even driving."

Their laughs filled the cabin and after a twenty-minute drive with talks about Lucky, Emmy's family farm and the Mills family in general, they arrived at the first store.

They found more items for Lucky at two more stores before sitting down in a small Italian restaurant for lunch.

"I can't believe you've never been to a karaoke bar. We'll have so much fun tomorrow." Errin took a big bite out of her pastrami sandwich.

"Didn't you hear me in the kitchen this morning?" Emmy raised a brow.

"Yep."

"So. There's your answer," Emmy said, forking her pasta.

Errin snorted, "You said 'spatu-laaaaahs', not quite an audition for The Voice in my book."

They both laughed until a guy held still at their table for two at the back of the restaurant.

"Emmy?" he said.

Errin looked up from her plate to the man who only had eyes for Emmy, to Emmy who turned white as a sheet. She still held her fork mid-air and her blue eyes stared back at the stranger.

"Hi. I'm Errin. And you are?" she said while sticking out her hand.

The man narrowed his chocolate eyes in Errin's direction before clearing his head by shaking it. He gave her a smile that didn't reach his eyes, but shook her hand in a firm grip.

"Kieran."

Emmy still hadn't uttered a single word.

Errin leaned over the table and said in a loud whisper to

Emmy, "I feel a joke coming. If you don't say something to Kieran, you're forcing me to—"

Kieran cleared his throat and said, "Emm. Can we talk? I—"

Emmy stood from the table and walked in the exit's direction. She didn't speak and just walked out of the door.

"What the fuck?" he said. And although he had a tanned, olive skin color, his agitation showed in his red cheeks.

"Yeah. I'm with you, dude. She's my ride and I have no idea where the fuck I am right now," she said.

"You're Emmy's friend?" he asked while raking his hand through his black wavy hair.

"Yes. But I have no clue what's going on," she said the last sentence as a question. She hoped he would fill in the blanks.

"Any idea where she's running off to?" he said as he sat down in Emmy's empty spot at the table, making the table for two seem rather small because of his sizable frame.

Emmy walked back to their table with determined steps, and her head held high.

"Errin, we're leaving. I've just paid, so we're ready to go."

"Please Emm. Sit down and talk to me," he said.

"Goodbye, Kieran."

Errin glanced over her shoulder at the raven haired man who they left behind, who was giving heated looks at Emmy's curvy backside. She walked with Emmy to the door of the restaurant but stopped dead in her tracks.

"I forgot my purse," Errin said.

"I'll wait outside," Emmy said as she kept on walking.

Kieran was staring at the table but looked up from the white and red-checkered tablecloth with hopeful eyes at Errin's approach, but slumped when he noticed it was Errin.

"I'm sorry, Kieran. I'm in the dark about what happened between you. But if you think you can fix this, more power to you."

Kieran observed her and it seemed like he was debating with himself what to answer her.

"She works at this pub, it's called The Lucky Irishman. If you can make her smile again, come around sometime."

She grabbed her purse and walked out of the restaurant. She wasn't sure if she'd done the right thing, but maybe it would help Emmy let go of the past she wasn't comfortable talking about.

"You ready?" Emmy asked.

"Yep."

As they walked over to the parked car, Emmy was silent and only glanced over at Errin once or twice. When they drove back to Lucky, Emmy snapped, "So, you're not even going to ask me?"

"Ha, as if. You'll only bite my head off, if I do. No, pretty little weirdo of mine, I'm not asking shit about this rendezvous. You'll tell me when you're ready." She smiled at Emmy.

Emmy sniffed and wiped a tear from her cheek. "Thanks."

"Do you want to hear my joke from the restaurant earlier?" Errin said.

"Fuck no. Please, I beg you. Stop with the jokes. I'd rather listen to Kieran's excuses than hear another Errin-joke."

"Hmm, okay. Well, we'll see. I think in time, the jokes on you."

"What did you do?" Emmy said in a high-pitched voice and swerved the car.

"Shit. Watch the road, Emm. Geez. Well, I might have mentioned the pub..."

"Fuck. I'm gonna cook you alive," Emmy said through gritted teeth. Errin couldn't help but laugh, but Emmy didn't join her.

"I'm dead serious, Errin. You have no idea what you've done," she said.

Errin swallowed and lowered her head. That was often her

problem, acting before thinking things through. "I'm sorry... I..." she said.

"Okay. If he comes to Lucky, you'll help me. You've made this mess, so least you can do is help me get out of it. Promise me you'll do whatever I'll ask of you. Or I will never trust you ever again," Emmy said, never once looking over at Errin.

"Shit. What the hell is this all about?"

"I... Okay, trust me when I say that I'll tell you—but not now. Seeing him after four years is... Oh my God, it's been four years..." she sucked in a breath and stared out of the window.

Errin figured they were lucky they stood stuck in traffic with the distracted Emmy behind the wheel. After a few minutes sitting in silence, Emmy said over her shoulder, "Okay. I'll tell you when you're back from Jersey. I'll need a few drinks for this story."

"You think I'm coming back here?"

"Never been more sure of anything in my life," Emmy said.

Austin

Brennan

20

"Walk on, bro." Ronan nudged Don's back with his rough hand. Donovan stood stock-still after taking two steps inside the crowded Thomas Tavern.

Loud music blasted in the bar next door to Lucky, while people threw shouts and hollers at two brunettes working the stage in the back.

It was Tuesday Karaoke Night and tomorrow night Errin would fly back to Jersey. Brennan, his brothers, and cousins were meeting up with the Walsh and Ryan girls after another day of hard labor.

Even though it pained him to see Lucky in such a state of decay, working on the rebuild of their family pub with his brothers and cousins was something special.

Errin had spent the entire day with Pops. His grandfather had their last day in Austin all planned out. He took her for a walk in the city and stopped for lunch at his favorite place, after Lucky that is.

Errin wanted to have drinks with just the girls at the beginning of the evening, so she could catch up with her sisters and friends. But now it was time for the guys to join, so they also could say their goodbyes to Errin.

"Fuck," Dunc said next to him. Brennan was trained to

oversee a crowded bar fairly quickly and froze in his spot when he noticed Errin. His eyes feasted on her as her body moved with perfect rhythm to the music as she stood on top of one booth.

Even in high heels, with little room to work with on top of a table, she out-danced all other women present. The sexy movements of her swaying hips made him swallow a lump in his throat.

She was dressed in a tight black dress that came mid thigh. But seeing Errin shake her butt on a table or any other flat surface in a bar was not some rare sight.

"What? She's enjoying her last night out in Austin."

Suddenly, Don walked through the crowd like he owned the place and walked with determined steps straight over to the back of the bar.

"No, not Errin. It's Kate and Bree, man," Dec said before following Donovan on his heels.

Brennan walked behind them and on his way over to the stage, he halted before Errin and pulled her into his arms in one big swoop. She yelped in surprise but didn't seem too bothered by his cave man ways.

"Hi, Gorgeous. Having fun?" he said, his mouth pressed against her ear.

"Yes! Did you see Kate? I'm so proud of her. She's always so shy and look at her—shaking her butt to that song. She's really making progress."

"What do you mean?" Brennan asked.

Errin leaned. "When we were young, she would hide her figure in oversized clothes and hated her thighs and butt. It wasn't so bad anymore before we moved out here, but I guess Donovan is helping her to appreciate her figure."

Brennan laughed. "Ha. Yeah, he appreciates her figure all right."

He walked them over to the stage and joined Dec and Don, who watched the girls like a hawk. Kate blushed like nobody's business but held on to her routine with Bree as they sang, "I like big butts and I cannot lie."

Declan cheered them on, and even Donovan grinned. As usual, his aloof brother only had eyes for his Kate and the moment the song ended, he held out his arms for Kate to jump into. She held on to him, wrapping her legs around his waist while he spoke into her ear. Her eyes widened, and she nodded.

Dec held out his hand for Bree to walk down the steps to the stage. Squirt was a bit wobbly in her purple high heels that matched her dress and nodded in thanks at Declan.

She accepted his hand, but the moment Bree was down, she let go and walked past him. Dec tried to halt her and as he laid his hand against her shoulder, but she sidestepped him and kept on walking to the booth where Kayla, Fianna and Emmy sat with the rest of his brothers and cousins.

Errin shifted in his arms and he let go of his girl. *Fuck. She's not exactly my girl, now is she?*

"I can't believe you did that! I'm so proud of you, sis," Errin shouted at Kate. Donovan held his arm around Kate's shoulder but smiled at Errin's words.

"Are you crying?" Kate asked Errin.

Errin wiped a tear away and said, "You really kicked some ass out there."

Brennan smiled as Errin boasted on and on about Kate coming out of her shell.

"Thanks, sis." Kate said and kissed Errin on her cheek.

"Let's get a drink," Declan said next to him. After being unmistakably dismissed by Bree, he was back to sulking. The group walked back to their booth, but Brennan held Dec by his shoulder.

"I take it you haven't had a talk with Bree yet?" Brennan said.

"Shit man. We've talked all right. We..." Declan moved in closer and as he lowered his voice he said, "We spend one night together at my place in September, and then again two weeks ago. Fuck, Bren. It was everything, man. But every time I think we can finally be together, she flips and storms out the door in the morning. She's been ignoring me for the past weeks."

"Why didn't ye tell me something had happened between yous earlier?" Brennan said. He was agitated with his brother as Declan normally told him everything of importance.

"She's spooked and she wants to keep it between us. She had ended things between her and her co-worker, but then again, she keeps talking to him.

"She doubts my feelings, but I'm going after what's mine. Ever since I've first laid eyes on her dark curly head..." Dec shook his head, smiling.

"Damn, is it even possible to find the love of your life when you're just eight?" Declan said.

Brennan slapped Dec's back, "I'm rooting for you, bro."

"Thanks," Declan said as they walked over to the booth.

Brennan took a seat next to Errin, and she took his hand in hers under the table. "How was it today? Got a lot of work done tearing the place down, before making it shine again?"

He glanced down at their laced fingers and squeezed once, just to remind himself she was real. He looked up at her. "It's going all right. We're even before schedule. Tomorrow I'll have a day off, so tonight and tomorrow I'm all yours," he said, waggling his brows. She smiled so coyly, he couldn't help but kiss her. Hard.

Out of breath, Errin said, "Bren... We have to stop kissing like this. If we don't stop now—"

"I know, Lips. I know... It's your last night out and you want to stay till the end." His eyes drifted over her face, taking in every detail.

He nuzzled her nose with his before kissing her again. His brothers' hoots and hollers traveled over the table suggesting for them to get a room somewhere, but other than flipping them off, he didn't let them ruin his night. Fuck them if they took offence.

He would take whatever Errin was giving him while she was still here. Like a bird waiting around for some crumbs, he was here for it all.

Errin kissed the corner of his mouth. "Mmm. I was thinking maybe another hour or so? And then I have a surprise for you."

His heartbeat raced, and he tried to hide his smile by taking a swig from his beer. She traced his lips with her thumb. "I love your smile," she said. "And sitting here... seeing you smile..." she shook her head like she had already said too much.

"What?" He squeezed her upper thigh under the table to encourage her to keep talking.

"It's silly."

"Tell me, baby girl."

"I'm just realizing why in the world you would ask me for a picture of a smile. I thought it was weird, you know? Out of all the things you could have picked." She grinned and rolled her eyes mockingly.

"But now... I want to take that smile off your face and carry it with me everywhere I go," she said as she traced his lips again with her thumb. "I..." she chewed the inside of her cheek before she averted her head.

He took her chin in his hand and brought her eyes on his again.

"Take out your phone," he said.

"W-what?" she blinked quickly, and he nodded. She took her phone from inside her black dress, where it rested over her left breast inside her bra. It reminded him of the night they kissed for the first time, after the Halloween party in Lucky. She unlocked her screen and handed it to him.

He opened the camera app and held out his arm. He flipped the screen so their faces appeared on the phone and put his arm around Errin's shoulders. He tugged her tight against him and she laughed out loud.

Her laugh was infectious, and he wholeheartedly joined her. He shot a few pictures and even took a couple while they kissed. He laid the phone on the table and grabbed Errin.

He placed her on his lap and as she turned in his arms; she laid her arms around his neck. She gave him a long, sensual kiss and the hollers from the others in the booth reappeared.

Errin smiled against his lips as she bit her bottom lip, and he couldn't stop the goofy smile that overtook his face. He never laughed or smiled as much as in the last few days together with Errin. The thought this would end tomorrow night pained him.

"Don't be sad, Bren," she whispered, suddenly eying him with worry.

"I can't help it, Lips."

"I'm thinking real hard over here to come up with a joke. Shit. Normally, they just pop up at the most awkward moments and I can't keep them from coming out."

"Maybe there are just no jokes. Maybe... it's fuckin'—"

"Oh! I got one!" she perked up on his lap, making his dick stand up at attention again.

"Shit. And so excited to tell me, too. Okay, come on. Break me heart, lass." He placed a hand on top of his heart while exaggerating his Irish brogue.

"Knock knock...." She grinned and waved her hand for him to answer.

"Who's there?"

"Single," she said.

He sighed and didn't respond. Fuck this stupid joke. She wanted to lighten the mood, but all it did was anger him. His nostrils flared at the thought of what came next after 'single who?'.

"Sorry," she whispered, "You're right. It's no joking matter. Come, we're going back to your place."

"You sure?" he shifted in his seat, already wanting to take her with him. She gave a curt nod before she leaned in and gave him a sweet kiss.

Don and Kate apparently had left already, and Kayla and Duncan were in the middle of saying their goodbyes. "I see you tomorrow, sis," Kayla said.

"Yes. See you at seven at Lucky's," Errin said as Kayla kissed her cheek. Brennan had offered to take Errin to the airport, but she wanted her sisters to bring her so they could have dinner together one last time before she left.

Errin stood from the table and said goodbye to Keenan, Aiden, Fianna and Emmy. After the obligatory "Good luck in Jersey" and "Call me when you're at Conner's," she took a dramatic bow like she just finished a show on stage and waved once more before turning her back to the booth.

Errin looked up at him as he took her hand. "What? There's only one first impression, but people often forget the last impression. Can't say this was leaving with a bang, but I'm not one to sneak out of the backdoor either." She gave him another devastating smile. Making his chest hurt.

They were on their way to the exit when they saw Bree and Declan sitting together at the bar. Dec leaned in and kissed Bree behind her ear.

"What do they put in these drinks at this joint? Everyone is acting all out of character tonight," Errin said, glancing over Brennan's shoulder at Declan. Brennan looked over and sure enough, Dec had his hand at the back of Bree's head and pulled her in for a kiss. Bree placed her hand on Dec's chest but didn't push him away.

"Get it, G.I. Joe," Ronan cheered his twin on by using his nickname.

Both Bree and Declan didn't respond, instead they deepened the kiss.

"Fuck. That's hot. Wanna go out of this place, Fi?" Ro threw out casually.

"In your dreams, asshole," Fianna responded while walking away from the bar with her drinks in hand.

Since the bar was right next door, Brennan and Errin walked into his apartment mere minutes later.

Errin had said nothing as they walked into the ravaged pub or as they stomped up the steps to his apartment. She didn't even cat-call when Dec was making out with Bree. And the awkward situation with Fianna and Ronan didn't get one joke out of her.

She walked into his kitchen and poured him a glass of milk and water for herself. His lip turned up as she'd remembered his habit of drinking milk before bed to calm his stomach.

They drank in silence with her leaning against the kitchen counter and him opposite of her against the kitchen table. Errin took a slight step and wrapped her arms around his waist to hug him close.

"You're making my shirt wet, baby girl," he said, his voice soft.

"Huh?" she backed away and inspected the tearstains. She tried to step away from him, but he took her hand and led her to the couch.

"You kick some Yankee arse, ye hear?" he said after they sat down next to each other. He wished it didn't need to end. But he was certain she'd regret it forever if she stayed for him. She stared at the bookshelves in front of them and didn't respond, as she was lost in her thoughts.

After a minute she wiped a stubborn tear from her cheek, righted her shoulders and said, "Okay, that's enough."

She walked over to his sound system and searched for something on her phone. After connecting the devices, she found what she was looking for and walked out of the living room.

She said over her shoulder, "I'll be just a minute. I promised you a surprise, remember?"

He smiled at her tactics to lighten this fuckin' shit mood. After five minutes of waiting on the couch, she shouted from his bedroom, "Okay. Bren, can you take a chair from the kitchen and sit on it in the living room, facing me?"

He took a condom from his wallet and put it in his front pocket of his jeans. Best to be prepared around Errin. He did as she asked and picked up a chair from the kitchen. The moment he sat down in the living room, he shouted, "Okay, done. I'm ready for you."

"Pssht. That's what you think." Errin came around the corner on the first tunes of 'New York, New York' by Frank Sinatra. She had her outfit down to a tee.

She'd tucked her wavy blonde hair under the typical old fashion man's hat. A slim tailor-made-suit covered her body. Well, her upper body at least.

The jacket of the black suit fitted her tiny waist and even gave her a small cleavage. Garter straps framed her firm arse, and she'd put on a lacy black thong. But her legs were bare. She sashayed over to him in the same sexy black heels she enticed him with earlier tonight.

"Yer right, Lips. I was nowhere near ready for this," he said before licking his dry lips.

Her eyes sparkled and a beautiful smile lit up her face, making her dimples pop even more. "Told ya!"

He shook his smiling head and spread his thighs. His instant erection made him uncomfortable as it strained against his dark blue jeans. Fuck. She even had a cute little bow tie to complement her outfit. He couldn't wait to fuck her wearing only those heels and bow tie. She strutted toward him on her makeshift dance floor, walked past him with her palm sliding over his shoulders, and halted behind his chair.

Her hot breath tickled his ear. "I've never done this before. You're my first, Bren." She licked him behind his ear, and he could just suppress a groan.

"Only you," she whispered.

She walked around him and halted a few feet before him. He reached out for her, but she smirked and shook her head. "Na-ah, naughty boy. No touching."

He groaned, as things were getting hard in more ways than one. She swiveled her hips and swirled around. His eyes went from her high heels to her calves, over her strong thighs to her firm arse cheeks. She might be a tiny thing, but she's strong as hell.

Errin kicked her heels in the air to each side, to the tunes of the song, and moved closer. She took the button of her jacket in both hands, while swaying her hips from side to side.

She dipped low with her knees pointing outwards. The see-through thong was by no means concealing and showed off her glistening pussy. He looked up just in time as she let the jacket fall to the ground.

She climbed onto his lap and straddled him. Her rosy-pebbled nipples drew him in and he sucked hard on one, before taking the other hard peak between his teeth for a loving tug.

His rough hands immediately slid to her cheeks. He started kneading her warm flesh to urge her to give them both more friction. A moan escaped her and he pulled her down once more. Errin rolled her body against him, and he leaned in to lick her collarbone.

"Ah, yes," she breathed. She took off her hat and threw it

through the room. Her honey strands tumbled down over her gorgeous body. She arched her back even further so he could explore her hard peaks with his tongue once again.

"This isn't how it's supposed to go..., Bren... I..." she whined but started riding against his dick with his jeans and her flimsy thong still between them. Her wetness coated his crotch and if he didn't cut this short, he would come in his jeans.

"Fuck the rules, Lips. Do you want this?" he asked with his blatant need marring his voice.

"Oh, yes... I want youuu," she shouted the last word, as he twisted her nipple between his thumb and index finger. She dipped her head to the crook of his neck and her short, hard breaths spurred him on.

He slid one finger under her thong and went in for the kill. After a few eager strokes on her clit, she rode him harder. She rolled her hips like he nestled deep inside of her with not his finger but his rock hard dick.

"I've got you, baby girl," he whispered against her lips. He let his hands go in between them to take his zipper down.

With her hands on his shoulders, Errin lifted just enough for him to tug his jeans and boxers down and take out his dick. He took the condom from his pocket and tore the foliage with his teeth. After sheathing himself, they both groaned in satisfaction as she slid down on his hard length.

"Yes. Yes. Yes."

Errin mewled with each downward motion. Her breath against his neck made him shudder.

"I'm so close," he said.

"I'm coming..." Errin moaned, her voice small and pained.

He closed his eyes and gave in to the tingles traveling up his spine. He bucked up into her while gripping her arse even harder. His thrusts were rough and fast.

The sound of Errin coming while she squeezed his dick with

her inner muscles, spurred his orgasm on. His cock throbbed once more before he released inside her.

She fell against his chest, and he kissed the top of her head. After a few minutes of catching their breaths, he whispered, "I'll miss you."

She chuckled and took his face in between the palm of her hands. She stared into his eyes. "You're just going to miss me riding you like some—"

"You damn well know that's not all there is to it, Lips," he griped and stood from his chair, with Errin still clinging to him.

She crossed her legs behind his back and he walked them over to his bedroom. He laid her down in the middle of his bed. "Going to make you remember me."

Austin

Brennan

21

Was that loud thumping all in his head or was someone banging on his door like his apartment was on fire?

Damn. Probably one of his brothers. They couldn't take a hint when he didn't react on all those texts and calls since Errin had left Austin last night.

"Go away," he boomed as he grabbed his pillow and placed it over his head. He cleared his throat, because man, did he have a dry mouth.

The opening of his front door and loud voices in his hallway alerted him of the fact that the whole cavalry had arrived. He should've known they would show up for an intervention. They finally had enough of his shit. He couldn't blame them. It was what he would've done, anyway.

"B. It's been a full 24 hours since she's gone. Go get your arse in the shower," Donovan said as he ripped the comforter from his stinking body.

"What time is it?" he groaned.

"Time to get your ugly white arse out of our sight, bro." Ronan snickered.

Right. He was still naked. He didn't bother to put clothes on when he'd grabbed a bottle of the finest whiskey from the kitchen to drown his sorrows. Pops would get on his case about the whiskey the minute he noticed it missing.

Brennan had gone home to an empty bed when Errin had fled the scene. He'd loaded her suitcases in Kayla's trunk, kissed Errin again for good measure, and waved goodbye like some kind of idiot. He couldn't find one good reason not to resort to drinking.

He'd reached out to her to see if she'd arrived at Conner's all right, and she'd texted, "Yes. Sleep tight."

Well, that was like a right hook to the chin. Couldn't she relay something more? No, she gave him three words. '*Yes*', '*Sleep*' and '*Tight*'. Fuck this shit. He wanted more. So much more. He yearned for something like, 'I miss you already'.

He shook his head, knowing that wasn't Errin. She needed to keep her distance. He got it, but at the same time he didn't get it.

"Fuck off," he muttered to his annoying brother, who kept on goading him.

"Go on, Bren. And if you ask nicely, I'll even shave that hairy arse for you." Ronan laughed.

"Leave me alone. Damn. My head hurts," he said, taking the pillow from his head.

Declan walked into his line of sight and crouched next to his bed. His worry lined face filled his vision and guilt ate at Brennan.

"I'm sorry for not answering any of you. I'll get my arse up and my shit together. Just... give me a minute."

"Fuck. I can't take this any longer. Anyone got a tissue?" Ronan said.

"Nobody cares if you cry, motherfucker. Shut yer face," Duncan said, making Brennan cringe as his head pounded in his skull.

"No, it's not for my face. It's for the back of his head. He's bleeding," Ro said as he walked closer and shuffled some hair on Brennan's head, making him cry out in pain.

"How in the hell did that happen?" Donovan said.

"Dunno..." Brennan groaned.

"This has got to be the worst I've ever seen ye. Fuck. Okay, Dec, grab some wet and dry towels. Ro, go see in the kitchen if there's a first aid kit somewhere," Don said.

"Sink..." he mumbled.

"What?" Donovan said.

"Under the sink," Brennan said.

"Right," Don said. "Okay, wait a minute before you move a muscle. We'll see to this cut. It doesn't look like it needs stitches, but we must make sure before you get out of bed."

"Geez. Just let me get up and—" he started before Ronan reentered the room and clanged the first aid box on his bedside table, making Brennan close his eyes and voice some profanities.

Declan walked over and cleaned the cut in the back of his head. The wet towel gave him a slight chill, but he tried to ignore it.

"Okay, most of it was dried up blood. You probably bled so much because you've downed a bottle of whiskey, which made your blood so thin you bled like a stuck pig," Dec said.

"Okay, G.I. Joe. Thank you for your crime scene analysis," Ronan snickered.

"Shut the fuck up," Dec said.

"Can all of you shut the fuck up? My head hurts," Brennan groaned.

"Does it hurt from your hangover or does your cut hurt?" Dec asked in his cop voice.

"Hangover. Now, I would like to go take a shower. So if any of you want to stick around for a show, be my guest. I'm getting my naked arse off this bed," He said.

Ronan held both palms up and took a step back, making him

bump into the closet. "What's up with this enormous bed in this room? Well, at least now you can get a smaller bed since Errin is gone."

"OUT." Brennan roared.

"You're such a dickhead, Ro. If you can't stop being a dick, you'd better get going," Declan said to his twin.

"Nah. If someone would say stupid shit under pressure, it was Errin. He likes it, remember?" Ro said and shrugged.

"Don't say another motherfuckin' thing about her." Brennan shouted before slamming the bathroom door closed behind him. Damn. He was certain it was coming. The hurt and the aching feeling of missing the other part of you that made you whole. But to actually feel his heart squeeze at the mere thought of Errin was terrifying.

Maybe that's why he drank himself into oblivion. He'd rather let the darkness thicken, closing in on him than to be aware of the longing for Errin that never would go away. No matter how hard he'd try.

After a quick shower where he unsuccessfully tried to remember how he ended up with a bump to the back of his head, he towel-dried his hair and changed in a pair of boxers, sweatpants and a white T-shirt.

Getting out of bed didn't mean he would go downstairs and face the rest of his family and start working. Not yet. First, he needed to talk to Donovan. If there was someone who could calm him, it would be him.

His brothers had made themselves comfortable on his worn brown couches and had turned on some sports channel. Donovan sat at his kitchen table, scrolling on his phone. Brennan walked past the twins on one couch and gave Dunc a chin lift in greeting. He walked over to Donovan and took a seat opposite of him.

"Not so long ago, you were the one who gave me advice

when I royally fucked things up with Kate," Donovan said. "I still can't wrap my head around how she forgave me, but if it weren't for my brothers pushing me in the right direction, I would still be one miserable fuck."

"Yeah, this is different D."

"How come?" his brother asked as he quirked a brow and sat back in his chair.

"I didn't fuck up. She's not mad at me and doesn't hate me. She's..." he sighed as he hung his head and traced a line on the oak tabletop with his thumb.

"She's just going on with her life. Doing what she's supposed to do—being free and acting like any twenty-six-year-old. It's not like I did something wrong. It's more that I will not stand in her way. She needs to do this, D."

Damn. That hurt. But saying it out loud made him see that he couldn't have done anything differently. He shook his head because surely she'd felt the same way? How could she not? It was the best damn thing he's ever had. How could she not feel the same?

"Bren," Donovan said to stop him from staring at the table.

"Yeah."

"Kate came home late last night after driving Errin to the airport. And she—"

Brennan didn't like the image of Errin stepping onto the airplane to fly out of his life, so he scraped his throat and said, "I can't do this right now, D."

"Well, let me say my piece and then I'll be on my way. We gave you one day, but tomorrow you'll get some normal clothes on and go downstairs. You'll work until your back hurts, until you're so fuckin' tired, you can't even see straight and pass out from exhaustion instead of a bottle of Jack.

"You'll do so for the next few days—make yourself get out of bed and be with your family. We'll help you get through this.

We're here for you, bro." Donovan knocked the tabletop twice and stood from his chair.

As Don walked past him he patted his shoulder and said, "And pick up the damn phone when any of us call you."

"Yeah, okay," he said.

Donovan left after talking a bit with their other brothers. Brennan stayed because it would be a dick move to go back to bed.

He walked over to sit next to Dunc on the couch where he had first held Errin after her fall from the stairs. He took a deep breath and fixated his eyes on the television screen.

"Can't believe they let him into the red zone. What a bunch of pussies," Ronan said.

The mutters of his brothers about the game were the background noise he needed to close his eyes to and let his thoughts run free. He laid his head back against the couch and took a deep breath. He didn't want to think. He wanted to forget.

When would this game be over? He didn't need to be babysat. Certainly not by his brothers. He would always be the one to check up on them, not the other way around.

Austin

Errin

22

"Shall I order us some water?" Conner asked. He patted her shoulder. Errin sat hunched over the bar and couldn't see straight.

Not like it took a lot for her to feel the effect of a cocktail, but this was ridiculous even for her light-weight-ass.

"I wanna go home," Errin said.

"Come, Bunny. We'll grab a cab outside and go home." He helped her down from her barstool by her elbow. Conner strolled to the side of the packed dance floor of the so called new it place for a Friday night.

They had been out for an hour, and she already had enough to drink. And enough of the place altogether.

Conner took their coats from a sturdy lady behind a desk and after another glance at Errin, he slipped them through the back entrance, leading them through the side ally, and in front of the main entrance of the nightclub where the taxi line stood.

"Fresh air will do you some good," he said while patting her arm that was hooked through his. She didn't answer him, but did her best at nodding.

"We've got three people in line before us, Bunny. I think it will take another ten minutes and then we'll get you home."

"Is the cab driving me all the way to Austin?" she said with a trembling lip.

"Aww, fuck. How much did you drink tonight, Bun?" he scolded. "Or did you take a drink from a stranger?"

She shook her head and the first tear went down over her cheek. Conner traced his index finger over her cheekbone and swiped it from her face.

"Is that what you call Austin now—home?" he asked as he pulled her in to hug her close.

She nodded against his hard chest and he held on tight and whispered, "Fuck."

"I miss him," she whispered back.

"I know, Bunny. I felt it the moment you stepped out of the plane and walked into my arms."

"You did?" she said as she backed up in her silver stiletto heels to look her brother in the eye.

"Yeah. Don't know what's so fucking special about Austin, Texas that got all my sisters hooked."

"It's the D." Errin hiccuped and glanced over her shoulder when someone snickered behind her.

"The what?" Conner asked with furrowed brows.

"The D. It's the dick that's so good, we're hooked. Got nothing to do with the weather, the friendly southerners or all that shite," Errin said.

She shivered because she forgot to wear her thickest coat over her spaghetti strapped silver paillette dress. The icy wind pained her face, reminding her November in New Jersey was so different from Texas.

"Shite, eh? Talking like a true Irish lass." He smiled before they took a few steps further in the line, now almost first in line.

"I still held hope that after a couple more days, you'd be reminded of your passion for dancing and you'd miraculously love it back home."

"I still love to dance, Con." Errin narrowed her eyes at him.

"To work out routines and express myself through dancing, it's what makes my heart beats faster.

"It's just that my heart is so heavy right now. I don't know if dancing can make this big lump in my chest beat faster or if it's only weighing it down more."

"Deep, sis." Conner laughed. "Ah, we're up next."

"Yeah well, I'll tell you something about deep, Brennan—" she started but Conner held up his hand, almost face palming her.

"Shut ye face, sis. Never, ever do I want to hear 'bout what ye were goin' to say," he said.

She almost doubled over from laughing. "Was just making conversation, Con."

"Well, converse about something else," her brother said.

"Okay. I loved how you threw in the Irish brogue there. Reminded me of Pops." And instantly the smile fell from her face again.

"Tell me somethin' funny, 'cause I'm standin' in line for a fuckin' cab, at one in the mornin', freezin' me arse off and me date is wishin' she was on the other side of the country instead of standin' here with me."

"Ooh, I can keep you warm, baby." A woman spoke from behind them. Errin looked over her shoulder and rolled her eyes at the brunette who eyed her brother. Conner winked at the woman but didn't give her a reason to come on any stronger.

"That's us," he said while leading them over to the cab.

After getting into the back of the cab and informing the driver of their destination, Conner began once more with prodding.

"How did it feel to be back on stage in the past few days?" he asked. Her brother's questions weighed heavily on her chest, like she couldn't breathe.

"Can you open the window for me, please? I think it's locked." Errin said to the driver after trying all the buttons.

"Yeah, but no puking in or against my car out of the window. If you gotta puke, get out the car," the driver said. He narrowed his blue eyes at her through the rearview window. The boyish man seemed to be her age, and why she even noticed that was beyond her.

She shook her head. "Not going to hurl, mister Detergent."

"What the f—"

"I'm sorry for my sister. She's a bit touchy right now."

"You're lucky it's only five more minutes."

"Yeah. Thanks," Conner said as he willed Errin with his eyes to keep her mouth shut.

After paying the cabbie and stepping out of the car, Errin walked together with Conner to their parents' home.

Conner lived in an apartment in Manhattan, but since their mother had persuaded Errin to stay with her parents for the first few nights in Jersey, he'd stayed with Errin tonight.

"So weird that we're here now and Kayla and Kate are still in Austin," Errin said. She shook off her coat and threw it on the first steps of the staircase.

"You still do that shit, eh?" Conner said as he waved at her coat.

"Hmm? Yeah. Sorry," she said, but made no effort to pick it up.

"Does Brennan know what kind of slob you are?" he said before chuckling and hanging up his coat at the rack in the hallway.

"Doesn't matter now, anyway, Con," Errin whispered as she passed him to enter the kitchen. She grabbed the ingredients for a hot chocolate and as expected, Conner joined her with their dads' favorite bottle of whiskey.

"I think we shouldn't break tradition, eh Bunny?" Conner

said. They both laughed out loud. The first time Errin drank alcohol was at twenty-one during the Thanksgiving dinner a few weeks after her birthday.

Their dad had the brilliant plan to spike their traditional hot chocolate with whiskey, and since Errin had been the last to turn twenty-one, all of her brothers and sisters could easily drink along. But not Errin. Not because it had been her first time, she would find out later on. She just couldn't hold her liquor.

The drinks were ready. Conner poured some whiskey in their mugs. Errin stirred with her spoon and took a sip. "Mmm, that's actually nice."

Conner took a spot at the large oak kitchen table that could host eight people. He took his usual spot at the far end, next to the fridge. While growing up, Errin always sat next to him until their mother Catherine pulled them apart. An incident with flying spaghetti and rolling meatballs had something to do with it. Errin grinned as she reminisced.

"Whatcha thinkin', Bun?" Conner said.

"We had some awesome times growing up here, didn't we?"

Conner took a gulp from his hot chocolate and nodded. "Yeah, sure did."

"I missed you all like crazy the first months I was in Austin. Like, I felt almost sick to my stomach from missing you guys."

Conner placed his arm over her shoulder. "It's okay if you miss him, sis. It's okay to have doubts."

"It's just that I've only done one show so I can't decide yet, but..." she sighed and took another sip.

"But what? Don't you like it as much as you'd used to?"

"I love dancing. But coming here and finding out I'm the understudy for the understudy is just... I don't know. It's not quite the gig I'd hoped it would be. But once you got your foot in the door, it gets easier to land other parts. It's just that I can't see myself doing this forever, you know? The girls are all so... superficial. So, New York."

"What's wrong with being New York?" Conner smirked.

"Nothing, I guess. But I miss the guys from the bar. That damn nagging Ed, the Mills cousins who never let me get on with my work without asking for a stupid joke. Pops... ugh, I miss Pops." She wiped a tear from under her eye.

"And?" Conner nudged her shoulder.

"And I miss Brennan," she confessed while nudging him back with her shoulder.

"In my line of work, I often come across people with regrets, Bun. People get sick or die without a moment's notice. Just like that—gone." He snapped his fingers.

"You're such a happy camper, Con." She scoffed.

"It's true. Come and do a night in the ER with me. After a day you'll agree with me you need to grab life by the balls."

"And squeeze them!" Errin shouted as she pantomimed squeezing a ball in her hand.

"Ouch, you're hurting my eyes, Bun." He laughed along with her.

After they'd calmed down he continued, "But grabbing life by the balls doesn't need to mean being on stage and dance. It might mean for you to take a chance on love. To go back on what you'd always believed to be your destiny and going after the love of your life instead. It might even scare you more."

She unlocked her phone for the millionth time in the past days to stare at the picture of her and Brennan at Thomas Tavern. It showed a smiling couple in love.

Yes, in love. The warmth in his eyes as he looked her in the eyes while laughing out loud, was a pure testimony of his feelings. Pops pressed during their farewell lunch about his grandson's feelings for her.

Not that Brennan tried to hide anything from her. She'd run

thousands of miles away from his intenseness, and it made her heart ache even more for Brennan.

A monumental part of her was missing. She'd left a piece of her heart in Austin that would always belong to that grumbling yet caring and sexy bar owner.

She hadn't been the fun loving, loud Errin in Jersey these last few days.

Instead, at her mother's kitchen table sat a watered-down version. An Errin that simply existed but didn't live like she grabbed life by the nuts.

She looked over at Conner and pantomimed squeezing again, making him shoulder check her once again.

"See? Even talking about him brings back the sister I used to know."

Austin

Brennan

23

"Can someone turn this shit down?" Brennan shouted upon entering the dust-filled pub with his hands packed with wooden panels.

He held the door open with his backside so Declan could squeeze himself through. Dec brought in the stacks of wood for Keenan's project, the recent custom made bar.

Aiden walked over from the far end where the pool tables normally stood, to where Keenan was hammering on the new booths on the long side of the pub. Aiden gave his brother a playful shove and turned down the music.

"Here you go, Cuz," Dec said.

"Thanks man," Keenan said as he perched himself off from the floor.

"You'll be deaf at forty," Brennan said as he joined his brother and two cousins.

Aiden snickered while taking the three upper stacks from his hands, but Keenan huffed a breath and said, "Ah, I take it ye still heard nothin' from her?"

"Fuck off," Brennan said.

"Why don't you just call her?" Keenan said.

Aiden elbowed his brother in the stomach to stop him from pressing further on the subject.

But Keenan continued, "I don't get it, man. I've never seen ye like the way ye were with Errin. Go get yer girl."

At the mention of her name alone, he wanted to put his fist through the fresh drywall. Brennan took a deep breath and said, "She's happy. She's finally doing what she's been wanting to do since she was a kid."

"He doesn't need to call her, boyo." Pops interrupted as he entered from the kitchen.

"He's gotta get his arse on the first plane outta here and go see our lass. If she still doesn't want to come home, then I'm never bringin' her name up again. Until then? Imma talk 'bout that sweet lass every single day. Remind him what he's missin' out on."

"Pops, I love ye with all of me heart. But if ye really plannin' to torment me—"

His grandfather held still beside him and ruffled his hair like he did when Brennan was still a pimpled kid.

"Pops..."

"No. You give this old geezer one good reason for stayin' here while the love of ye life is poutin' on the other side of the country."

"I promised her, dammit!" Brennan said, but suddenly jerked from his grandfather's hold and locked eyes with him. "Poutin'?"

"Sure is." Pops' lips turned up at Brennan's hopeful voice. "Talked to her me self. She misses us, boyo. She misses ye arse."

"She said that?" his voice came out even more high pitched.

"Phhst. No need, Brennan, me boy. It's clear as day. The lass loves ye and misses ye." Pops folded his still brawny arms above his round belly. His striped shirt stretched even more by the movement.

"I figured as much. Pops," he held up his hand because his grandfather was itching to interrupt him. "I promised her I would never hold her back. She's meant to be on that stage, Pops. I refuse to be the reason for her to walk away from her dreams. She would only end up hating me."

Brennan groaned as Sean Jr. walked into the pub. His entry reminded Brennan that he was discussing his non-existing love life in front of his brother, cousins, and now even his father.

"I'm done talking," Brennan said.

"Okay, then start listening," Sean Jr. said as he walked to the dusty folding table in the middle of the construction site. He placed a bottle of whiskey on top of the wobbly table and clanked several glasses next to the bottle.

"I'm not doing this with you," Brennan said as he narrowed his eyes at his father's back while he was busy pouring each a glass. Everyone else walked over to his father, calling it a day.

Brennan glanced around the bare room. It was Saturday and his cousins already completed the stripping part of Lucky and were now in the middle of building up the place.

His uncle Niall had decided hours ago he was done for the day, leaving the young hounds to wrap things up for the night.

Niall would retire soon, leaving his construction company to Keenan and Aiden. He'd told them to work in the pub and he'd be in charge over the kitchen.

Brennan figured his uncle wanted to see if they could hack it on their own. They were ahead of schedule, so at least there was nothing wrong with his cousins' work ethics.

Brennan glanced over his shoulder and met his brother's scrutinizing stare head on.

"What?" Brennan barked.

"*What?*" Dec said as he raised a brow.

"Is that really all you're gonna say?"

Brennan turned around to face Declan, and before he could answer him, Dec already started again.

"It's like WWIII out here. Or another fuckin' cold war. Come, drink with us."

"You know I have my reasons, Dec," he said.

"Son. Ye need to let me talk for a sec here," Sean Jr. said as he grabbed some white plastic chairs and placed them next to the others who already had sat down. Sean Jr. let out a exasperated sigh while sitting down on a stool.

"We haven't always seen eye to eye—" Sean Jr. said.

Brennan snorted while picking up a few strayed coasters from the floor and letting them go through his fingers. The silence between him and his dad weighed heavily like a dark cloud above their heads, but in the end, he couldn't help but glimpse at his father.

"Ye may think ye know everything there is to know about what happened after yer mom died but..."

Sean Jr. swallowed a big lump in his throat and continued, "Yous, nor any of me boys get how it feels to get yer heart ripped out from yer chest, leavin' ye paralyzed from this achin' pain. So much so, that ye can't even function.

"I couldn't take those green eyes of some of me boys without picturin' Edith... without gettin' pissed she wasn't with us anymore. She should've been there for you kids when you were growin' up, she should've been—"

Brennan stormed over to where his father sat with his grand-father, cousins, and brother. Like a damn reunion. Was this how it would go down between them? He wanted to talk? Bring it on.

Brennan sat down next to his father and turned his body to his father. He leaned in and said in a dead calm voice. "You should've been there for us. Gettin' pissed at mom for dyin' and not bein' there for us is makin' me fuckin' blood boil. Ye were alive and kickin' and still wasn't there for us. So help me God, one more word about mom and I'll—"

"Boyo. Son. I've had it. We gonna talk things through for

once and for all." Pops slammed his calloused fists on the squeaky table and stood with the biggest scowl he'd ever witnessed on his grandfathers' grumpy face.

Pops narrowed his eyes. "Aye, Boyo. Ye can snort all ye want. I can handle me self. Ye may treat ye father like shite for the last twenty years, but the day ye think ye can take on this old man it's gonna cost ye. Imma take me cane and go after yer arse. Ye won't be sittin' down for a month, ye hear?"

Aiden choked on his whiskey, making Keenan clap his back until he quieted.

"I didn't mean to disrespect you, Pops. I love you," Brennan said. He'd subconsciously taken the stack with coasters with him and was now pulverizing the coasters, one by one.

Pops' hand rested on Brennan's back and somehow stroked the tension away. Brennan righted his shoulders and glanced over to his dad who poured the three generations of Mills men another hefty glass with the amber liquid. Brennan couldn't believe he would share a drink with his old man, when he'd said such hurtful things about his mom.

Pops picked up his glass and said, "I'd like to propose a toast. To us all sharing a drink as a family, and my son and grandson finally letting go of the past."

"Things ain't that easy, Pops. If ye think we're goin' to simply hash things out over a bottle of booze, yer mistaken. I've got twenty years of anger inside of me. It's best if I take it out on Ronan in Duncan's Dojo—" Brennan said.

He took his glass to his mouth, letting the liquid warm his throat, as he not only swallowed the whiskey but also his pride.

Brennan needed closure, he was aware of that fact, even though he wasn't open for it right now. He caught sight of the worried lined eyes of Pops next to him.

Pops shook his head and after downing the rest of his whiskey; he clanged his glass on the table.

"Aye, Imma 'bout to lose me temper here."

"Listen to them, Bren. There is nothing worse than finding out your time with someone is up. All your hopes and dreams for the future... gone with the flick of a wrist. Finding out you can never go back and do things over..." Keenan shook his head and sighed.

"Just... look at the horizon. Go forward and don't hold yourself back by living halfway in the past."

Keenan stood from the table and said, "I'm going home. Get me some cuddles from Tommy."

"I'm coming with you, bro. See ya'll tomorrow," Aiden said as he stood from the table.

Aiden and Keenan walked into the kitchen, and the swishing of the swinging doors in their wake was the only sound in the now silent pub.

"Okay, so like Keenan said just now... I think we can all agree that if one of you two walks out of the door right now and get hit by a bus, the other would always regret to never have the chance to get certain things off his chest.

"So perhaps, because I feel a lot of tension coming from you, Bren, it's best if you start? Throw it all out for once and for all?" Declan said. Always the negotiator.

"Okay. You all asked for this. So don't come at me after this. Okay?" Grunts and hums met Brennan's words.

"So..." he said as he glanced at his father again. "I think ye did a shit job as a father and I can't help but want to slam me fist in ye laughin' mouth. Each... and... every... time... I see ye."

He swallowed the rest of his whiskey in one and slammed his glass back at the table. Damn, it felt good saying that shit out loud.

Perhaps the one thing he hadn't been open and honest about was the hurt he felt since growing up without a mom, or a dad. It still ate at him, making him feel like that fourteen-year-old boy who lost his mom and had to step up for the rest of his younger brothers.

"No matter what happened in the past, you've got to work this out," Declan said.

"This is our dad we're talking about. And if that isn't enough incentive for you to figure things out, take a good look at our grandfather. If you can't see the hurt behind his eyes, then you're also blind as hell."

"I'm doing all right, bro. Don't really need that womanizing, fake—" Brennan said.

"Don't ye think I don't realize I fucked up? All me boys still don't come to me for anythin'. Always come to ye to ask what ye would do. Never askin' their dad for advice. And it's a damn shame because every drunk in Austin is sharin' their life story with me."

"It's ye own fault. Ye never bothered with us, *with me*! And now we're all grown ass men, ye want to have the same relation I have with me boys."

"*Yer* boys?" Sean Jr. roared, his face red and his eyes ablaze with anger.

Brennan stood from the table and spoke in a dead calm voice while thumbing his chest. "Yes. My boys. I raised them. I helped Duncan to get into the dojo so he could work off his anger. The anger he had because he couldn't understand why his dad spent almost every day of the week hanging around a goddamn bar.

"Or did you show up at school when Ronan got suspended for punching some punk kid in the nose after he said something about our mom dying and you going on a fuck-'em-all-spree at the bar? Well?"

Sean Jr. shook his head while staring at the tabletop. Pops stood and placed his hand on Brennan's shoulder to gently nudge him to take his seat again.

"We all know how much ye did for all ye brothers, boyo.

Sean knows too. That's why he's so... pissed. Guess he's mostly pissed at himself. He got a wrong way to go 'round things. But we hear ye."

Brennan slumped in his seat while Pops had his arm around his shoulders. He was talking to him, soothing him. Ah, shit. Was he crying?

Sean Jr. got up from his seat and hunched in front of Brennan. He grabbed Brennan's closed fists on top of the table and engulfed them in his own.

Brennan took one hand from under his fathers' hands and angrily wiped the tears from under his eyes. He cleared his throat and said, "Shit. This is ridiculous. I never cry."

Sean Jr. chuckled and held up his palms at Brennan's narrowed eyes. "Ye found a fine thing in Errin, son. Hold on to her. I would do anything to get me Edith back. No matter how many women passed after her, I still haven't forgotten your mother, boys. If ye find that kind of love, ye hang on to it."

Brennan nodded and didn't argue with his father. That had to be some kind of improvement, right?

Sean Jr. stood and grabbed his son's cheeks so he could lock eyes with him. "I loved Edith with all of me heart. I went down a real dark path when the love of me life died.

"Tried to shut down all emotions by drinkin', fuckin' and runnin' away from me boys—from all that reminded me of her. But I love ye. It's breakin' me heart knowin' how we are together. And I know it would've broken Edith's heart if she was still among us."

Brennan glanced over at Pops, who was silently crying next to him. They hugged each other close and Brennan said against his dad's ear, "I respect ye for comin' out and sayin' what I've waited so damn long on. It's gonna take some time. Hope ye can give me that."

Sean Jr. nodded and took out a handkerchief from his

trouser pocket. He clapped Brennan on his back before letting go to wipe his tears away. Brennan turned and hugged his grandfather.

"I love ye. I cannot thank ye enough for always having me back and watchin' out for me—and the rest of us. Even now, when I was too stubborn to listen, ye guided me in the right direction. Thank you."

Pops cleared his throat and said, "Took ye long enough. Was 'bout to bind yer arse to the chair to make ye listen."

They chuckled at his words, and Brennan gave his grandfather a peck on the cheek. Brennan let go of his grandfather and turned his attention to his brother. He grabbed Declan by the shoulder and hugged him close.

As they slapped each other's back, his dad said, "Right. Cheers to the Mills men."

Pops slapped Brennan on his back and said, "Imma goin' get sloshed. Nothin' is gonna take me out of this mood for a looong time," he said as he picked up his whiskey and saluted them all before taking a hefty gulp.

"Aye, never tasted better. I'll tell ye."

"Mom? Dad? What are you still doing up?" Errin had forgotten in the past months, while staying in Austin, that her parents always went to bed at ten.

After she'd woken up the whole house right after her first show on Thursday, she made a promise to herself to sneak into the house after work.

Catching Caroline and Jack Walsh still sitting at the kitchen table at midnight was unexpected.

Even more unexpected was seeing Pops sitting opposite of them, smiling at her like nothing had happened.

Like she hadn't left his grandson. Like she hadn't left the pub on such short notice for a part in a musical up north. Sure, she'd talked every other day with Pops on the phone. But seeing the massive grumpy bear broke the dam.

She sprinted around the table and jumped into his heavy arms. She ugly cried as her entire face twisted in a battle of smiling and crying at once.

"What are you doing here, Pops? I can't believe it you're really here!" She squeezed her arms tighter around his colossal frame. His belly stood in the way of a full hug, and his familiar grumbling voice was like music to her ears.

"I'm here to bring back our lass," he said.

Her father Jack stood from the table and Errin knew what he was going for in the kitchen.

As Jack turned and walked back with the whiskey, Pops said, "Aye, that's right. Let's share some drinks, Jack. And then tell me what ye would say to me taking Errin back with me?"

She snuggled into his arms and pressed her cheek against his chest, breathing in the familiar scent of cigars as it enveloped her. She made no attempt to let this Mills man go. One had been bad enough.

"Aye, lass. Ye missed me, eh? Missed ye too," he said as he patted her back.

"Now, let's have a seat," he said.

"You're taking me with you to Austin?" she said, glancing up next to him.

He snorted. "I like the way ye think. But first I have to ask ye, are ye done with all this? Can't have ye hurtin' me boyo any more."

She let her head fall down and stared at the oak tabletop. Pops lifted her chin with his calloused hand and said, "Ye looked so beautiful up there. It was a sight to behold. Ye definitely belonged there. Well, maybe not that exact podium, but definitely on a stage."

"You were there? Did you see the show?" she asked.

"Aye. Was only lookin' if I could see ye on stage. Why aren't ye more on the stage?" he said with his eyes narrowed.

She smiled, "I only got an insignificant part, Pops."

"That's plain stupid. The others couldn't dance for shite," he said before taking a hefty shot.

"Pops..." she tried, but he patted her arm and looked up as her three brothers entered the kitchen.

"Did I miss the memo of a family meeting somehow?" Errin said.

"No." Conner grinned. "Nobody told yer arse. What kind of intervention would that be, sis?"

She furrowed her brows and said, "Intervention?"

"Conner..." Her mother said, her voice stern.

"Yeah," Conner said. "Welcome to the intervention of Errin Walsh. The girl we all love so dearly, but who is as stubborn as a donkey's arse."

He waved his arms around dramatically. "We all see her wither away before our eyes and this has got to stop, dammit."

"Con. Take a seat, and for once, shut up," her dad said. He poured whiskey for her brothers.

"He's full of shite, sis," her brother Evan said. "You're not withering away. But you're damn well unhappy, that's for sure."

The chocolate haired Walsh brother resembled her sister Kate the most. Well, by appearances only.

Evan was a beautiful man with his dark hair, chiseled jaw and eyes so strikingly blue, they almost seemed fluorescent. But he also had a forceful personality and always spoke his mind, unlike their sister Kate.

"Ev..." she glanced at her glass in front of her and gathered her thoughts. "It has nothing to do with you. I hope ya'll know this."

"Ya'll?" Her oldest brother Calum snorted.

Ha, she'd never once said ya'll in the entire time she'd lived in Texas. Where the hell did that sudden Southern drawl come from?

Errin looked up at the smiling faces around the table. Her mother coaxed her to continue talking by nodding her head, and as she looked over at her father, he smirked knowingly at her from behind his glass of whiskey.

Errin cleared her throat. "So you all knew—even before me, that this wouldn't work out?"

"Sweetheart, you've been heartbroken since you've said goodbye to Brennan," her mother said.

"You've lost five pounds in the last few days because you're too sick to your stomach and you just won't eat." Her mother leaned over the table to squeeze Errin's hand.

"I'm sorry, mom. I hate to worry you," Errin said, giving her mother a smile that didn't reach her eyes.

Conner padded his flat abs and said, "Yes, Bunny. Please go back to stuffing your face like you normally do. I've been picking up all your leftovers, and it's showing."

Evan gave the back of Conner's head a playful smack.

Calum leaned his powerful forearms on the tabletop and said, "So, what's the plan, sis?"

"Aye, yer aware there are dance studio's or other dance gigs in Austin?" Pops said.

"Dance gigs?" Errin snickered as she glanced up at him.

"Don't act like ye don't know what I mean. Ye can teach even old Ed to do a perfect waltz. I saw how happy that naggin' man made ye by followin' yer lead around the pub. Yer a born teacher. That's for sure."

He smiled at her.

"I'll always love ye, dear lass. If ye love me grandson or not, I'll always be there for ye. But if ye love him, don't let ye stupid pride get in the way. It's okay to change yer mind—to choose love and to place yer own happiness above a dream ye had when ye were young. Maybe yer meant to do other things with yer gift. Because I get it's a gift. Ye can entrance anyone by dancin' like ye did tonight."

Errin nodded as he caressed her cheek. He took a deep breath and said, "If ye still want me to give ye that gobble, ye better come back with me," he said with a wink.

Brennan filled another couple of pints of draft beer and placed them in front of Keenan. He nodded after his cousin had thanked him.

Keenan came to opening night with a girl that eerily resembled Errin. Not quite, because she was as dull as dishwater, but the honey blonde hair and blue eyes irked him.

"Brennan, we need you for a sec!" Sean Jr. shouted from the other end of the bar.

"Okay. Coming." He finished stacking the few clean beer glasses left.

He walked through the crowd, and a few regulars padded him on his back. Ed said, "It looks so good, son. I told Sean Jr. he didn't need to worry so much."

Brennan laughed and said, "Yeah. Keep tellin' him that."

Every barstool, chair and booth was filled.

This opening night was for invites only. Everyone that had worked so hard to make this opening possible was here. His family and friends.

Friends of friends. Everyone he remotely liked, but there was one person missing. It seemed to become a recurrent exponent in his life, always acknowledging the fact that she was missing.

It had been a week since he last seen her, but the pain in his chest whenever he thought of her didn't lessen.

He shook his head and walked over to his dad who climbed on top of one of the pool tables. His dad stood with the microphone in his hand, but since the pub was full with loud talking people, nobody paid attention at first.

Fianna took her fingers in her mouth and gave a shrill whistle, silencing almost everyone at once.

"Thanks dear. I would like to take a moment to thank everyone present. Everyone who has worked so hard these past few weeks to make Lucky an even better version of itself. I want to thank my oldest son, Brennan, who'll take over from me. I couldn't be more proud of him. He'll do things in his own way, and I'm certain it will be a tremendous success," Sean Jr. said, taking a sip from his beer as the crowd clapped and hollered.

"And I want to thank my father, Pops, for everything he has done for me and for my boys when things were tough at home. He was the one who guided my sons when I..." Sean Jr. wiped a single tear from his cheek and shook his head.

"Enough of that. I want everyone to lift their glass and to toast to the new Lucky and the new owner, my son Brennan."

Everyone cheered, and Brennan felt the need to say something, since they trained all eyes on him.

Although he wasn't a man of many words, tonight was special, so he climbed next to his dad on top of the pool table and hugged his dad. Applause erupted and as he glanced down to the floor, he saw his brothers watching them with teary eyes.

He cleared his throat and took the mic from his dad. "So, this is something I never thought I would do, but thank you, dad."

Sean Jr. wept and grabbed his shoulder to hang on to him.

"You made this place a home. Not only to our family, but also for so many others. I'm proud of you for all that you've done for Lucky, and I am thankful you're giving me the opportunity to take over."

He stopped before he broke down. The tears were pricking

behind his eyes. He kissed his dad on his cheek as they hugged it out.

Someone had turned on the music again, and he went back to his station behind the bar. After serving two orders, the DJ turned the music off mid song and Brennan looked up with narrowed brows.

What was wrong with the guy? Why was he silencing the crowd? He observed the customers and sure enough, their attention was once more focused on the pool table.

"Hi everyone! I wanted to take this opportunity to wish Sean Jr. a happy retirement and to congratulate Brennan. I know you'll do exceptional things with Lucky and it will be a huge success."

What the fuck?

Was that Errin on top of the pool table? She was standing in a sexy dark green halter dress that hugged her small waistline. She'd braided her warm blonde hair to the side, and loose strands framed her high cheekbones. She seemed flustered with a cute red blush that started on her throat to her cheeks.

She looked over and stared directly into his eyes from the other side of the pub, and he walked from behind the bar to get to her. She was here, and he was sure to get as close to her as possible.

"Now, I'm aware most people expect me to throw in a joke here or there. And who am I to disappoint, so let's go!" she said.

Ronan placed his hands to his mouth and shouted from the crowd, "Fuck no. Don't do this."

She flipped him the bird and Brennan laughed at her feisty attitude. She just took no shit from no one. As he walked through the crowd, several encouraging slaps fell to his back. He held still next to his brothers, in front of the makeshift stage.

"Did you ever hear the joke about the bunny that went to

Jersey to dance? Turned out she could only hip-hop," Errin said
with a smile in her voice.

People laughed, but Ronan shouted, "That's all you got?"
Brennan jabbed him in the ribs, making Ro laugh.

Errin searched the crowd and when their eyes connected
again she said, "Okay, not my strongest joke. I agree. Damn,
you're a tough crowd tonight. Here is another one. It will be my
last, so stop scowling, Brennan Mills."

He wasn't even aware he was scowling, and after blinking
once, he gave her a smile.

"I have one especially for you, okay? So bear with me," she
said.

She was really here.

Back in Austin.

Back in Lucky.

Was she here to stay? Or was she going to torture him by
coming over for a day or two before walking out of his life again?

"What does a girl say after she goes cross-country to pursue
a dancing career?" she started and paused before adding, "Well?
Do you have any idea?"

He moved from his brothers to a stop in front of the pool
table. Their eyes connected once more and his ears drummed.
So close. He just had to stretch his arms and then he could
finally have her in his arms again. Where she belonged.

"I'll tell you. She would say she'd made a mistake. And that
she'd been an absolute fool to run away from her feelings for the
most sexy and caring man alive."

He climbed on top of the pool table and took her in his arms.
She let out a squeak and her minty breath tickled his neck as
she giggled.

She seemed smaller than the last time he held her in his
arms. Emmy would have to make a lot of barmbrack to give his
girl her delicious curves back.

He looked down into her eyes as she whispered, "I've been a total idiot. I've missed you like crazy and—"

His heart jumped out of his chest as he leaned in and kissed her. Finally. She moaned against his lips and he held on to her narrow hips.

The bar erupted in one enormous cheer. Beer coasters and even splashes of beer and other thrown drinks made them all sticky and wet.

She giggled against his wet shirt. "I love you, Brennan Mills. I absolutely fucking love you."

"I love you too, Lips. God, how I've missed you."

He took her in his arms and jumped off the pool table. She held tight and stuck her head in the crook of his neck to shield her face from another couple of beer showers. He didn't care. He had his girl back in his arms and nothing else mattered.

He walked them over to his apartment and after opening his door; he locked it behind them.

"Fuck, Lips. This..." he shook his head and took her over to his bed where he sat her in his lap.

She still had her arms around his neck and giggled. She kissed him and whispered once more, "I love you."

With euphoric wonder, he searched her light blue eyes for the truth in her words. He slowly let go of his breath when he established the raw honesty in her words. His chest expanded and goosebumps traveled over his arms as he held her close to him.

In one brisk move, he took her from his lap and laid her on top of his comforter.

"Ah, Brennan. I'm making your bed all dirty with beer stains."

"Fuck, I forgot. Come, let's get cleaned up," he said.

"So we can get dirty again?" she said while waggling her brows.

He laughed and slapped her tiny arse as she walked in front of him to the bathroom.

She turned around and said, "It's the same spot where you took me for the first time, Bren."

How could he forget? Every time he'd walked into his bathroom, he'd thought of her. While shaving in front of the mirror, he pictured her standing there in his rolled up sweatpants and borrowed shirt.

"Yeah, but this time, I'm going to take my time with you."

He took the halter from her tight green dress and opened it from the back. He let it fall down in the front, exposing her breasts.

Her rosy nipples pointed at him and as he leaned in, the smell of stale beer filled his nostrils. "Fuck, you smell like a can of beer."

"Such a romantic." She snorted. "You're not smelling any better, believe me."

He opened the shower stall behind him and turned on the spray. After checking the temperature, he glanced over his shoulder and was just in time to see Errin step out of her last pump. She stood buck naked with her chest puffed out and her hands on her hips.

"Aren't you going in the shower?"

"Yes. Just had to make sure the water isn't too hot. Relax, Lips. I'm getting under the spray with you," he said while roaming his eyes over her tempting body. Yep, definitely needed to give her some Full Irish breakfast too. What was she eating up north?

She took a few steps closer to him and grabbed the hem of his black Lucky shirt. He let her pull it over his head. He toed off his shoes and made a work of his jeans and socks. She passed him to go under the spray and slapped his naked arse.

He chuckled and moved even faster to join her. After taking

the shower gel in his hand, he smeared her entire upper body with the gel. He placed the bottle back on the ledge and engulfed her breasts with his hands.

"So beautiful. I can't believe you're back. You're back, right?" he eyed her as he asked her.

"Yes..." she breathed.

"I can't hear you, Lips. Say what I want to hear," he said as he twitched her nipples.

"Aaaah, yes. I'm here and I'm back for good," she moaned.

"Tell me more," he demanded as he let his hands wander her body, going over her back to her arse and around to her flat belly. She was lost in his touches, so he tugged her belly button piercing to bring back her attention to his question.

"I want to stay with you here. I..." she panted as he flicked her clit with his thumb.

"And?" he asked while sticking two fingers in her pussy.

"Yes! Oh yes! I—" he took out his fingers and locked eyes with her.

"Are you ready for me? Are you going to let me take care of you?" he said.

She grabbed his shoulders and hooked one leg over his hip as she moved against his fingers back at teasing her clit.

"I want you Brennan and I don't care any more. I want only you and I love you," she moaned.

"Good," he said. He lifted her up behind her thighs and slammed her back against the shower wall. He took his dick and entered her treacherously slow while not once breaking eye contact.

"I love you too. So, so much," he said while rocking in and out of her.

Their tongues plagued each other in a teasing duel. He moaned as she grabbed his hair in her fist and pulled.

"I'm coming, Bren. I... I can't hold on... please, you..." she moaned.

After picking up the rhythm, the tingles traveled his spine and made him aware of the nearing end.

"Yes. Come with me, aaaah." He groaned.

Her walls clamped down on him, and they came together. She held back her head to wash her face under the stream and when she turned her head to him; she bit her lip and smiled. His heart skipped a beat. That damn smile.

Austin

Epilogue
26

"What do you mean, you're late?"

"You damn well know what it means."

Errin stopped dead in her tracks in the kitchen with her tray full of dirty dishes.

She was trying to put the voices to the people she was certain she knew, but couldn't place yet because of the loud conversation in the pub on the other side of the doors.

It was Thanksgiving and two days after opening night. Not only Mills men and Ryan women, but now even the complete Walsh family swarmed Lucky.

"Is it mine?"

The sound of a hard slap followed by a male grunt came from behind the back door to the back alley. She shouldn't be listening in on this conversation, but it was so juicy. Who in their right mind would walk away, right?

"Can you blame me? We fucked twice, Bree. You said you wanted nothing to do with me and you're still talking to that douche."

Oh, shit. Bree and Declan. Oh my God, she's pregnant?

"Yes. *Talking*. Moron. Not fucking," Bree sneered.

"Well, how am I supposed to know?" Declan said and Errin winced.

"I'm only telling you this because it's the right thing to do—" Bree started before Declan interrupted her.

"What do you mean? If you think I'm the father—"

Errin clanged a few dishes on the worktable, making her presence known. Where is Emmy when you needed her? She shouldn't leave Errin alone for this. This is going to be super awkward, but here goes nothing. Errin walked to the back door and stuck her head around the corner.

Bree stood with one hand on her flat belly, and Dec sat on the bench against the wall.

"Hey, you guys. Everything all right here?" she said.

Declan narrowed his eyes at her and said, "Not a word. I know how you operate, Errin."

"Dec. What is wrong with you? Don't talk to her like that! She's your brother's girlfriend for crying out loud." Bree defended her.

"Well, if Errin heard us, the news will travel our families faster than the speed of lightning. And since you were nice enough to spring this news on me with both our families, sitting only a couple of feet away—" Declan said.

"Ah, shut it Dec. I didn't mean to throw it all out like this," Bree said while stomping a few steps away from Declan.

"So yeah, I'm asking you, Errin. Please, not a word," he said in a much softer voice.

"I'm telling Brennan. Because we keep no secrets between us. But other than him, not a word from me." Errin faked zipping her lips and took a step back from the doorway.

Bree nodded at Errin and turned back to Declan. Like her pants were on fire, Errin went past their families who were all stuffed with Thanksgiving food, straight up the stairs to her and Brennan's apartment.

Because that's what it was, more or less. She hadn't moved in officially, but she spent every night there in his ridiculously enormous bed.

"Bren," she said as she walked into the apartment. He stuck his head from the fridge and said, "Damn. All those leftovers. We'll be eating cranberries for weeks on end."

"What's wrong, filly?" he said as he cocked his head. Okay, how was she going to tell him this news? Her palms were sweaty, and she rubbed them against her deep purple dress.

"I just overheard—"

"You can't do this every time you hear stuff at the bar, Errin. People need a place to vent, to tell you their story. You can't tell anyone whats' been said—"

"Bree and Declan are going to have a baby!" she blurted.

"No way." Brennan let a dish fall to the ground, those horrific green peas rolling everywhere. Why he even bothered to keep that dish for later was beyond her.

"Yes way. I just overheard them talking in the back alley. Declan got pissed I overheard them, but I just had to tell you. I'm sorry. I won't tell anybody else, but I needed to tell you," she said.

"No, it's okay. Oh, shit," Brennan said as he took Errin and placed her on his lap and sat down at the kitchen table.

She nestled herself and after a few minutes of silence, she couldn't hold it in any longer. "The stork is the bird that helps deliver babies. What bird helps prevent pregnancy?"

Brennan groaned but said, "Okay, I'll bite. What bird?"

"The swallow," she said, but didn't laugh at her own joke—for once.

28

EXCERPT DECLAN - BOOK 4

P ROLOGUE - BREE
March—nine months ago
Tonight's the night. No more self-doubting and pussyfooting. Bree checked her lipgloss once more in the vanity mirror of the sun visor, flicking her tongue over her pearly whites. She righted her shoulders, took a deep breath and traced her fingers over the car door panel in search of the handle.

The Texas heat engulfed her rich dark curls right after exiting her beat-up purple sedan. After a few short brushes through her bouncy strands with her fingernails, Bree gave up the effort to tame her hair. She'd parked in her usual spot; behind Dec's black Chevy on his impeccably clean drive way. How did he find the time to pull out all those weeds and tackle the overgrown mess since he was still renovating inside?

She'd been here almost every day and most nights for the past three months. At first, she'd helped Dec clean out all the junk left behind by the former owner. The house had been a steal, but not without reason. It had been a dump. A smelly, dingy two-story house in southeast Austin.

Never one to shy away from hard work, Bree even assisted the Mills brothers and cousins wherever she could as they helped Dec in remodeling the two-story house. It had been a lot of fun learning some tricks of the trade from Dec's cousins Keenan and Aiden who worked construction for their father's construction company.

Bree used her hand, shielding her light blue eyes from the lazy evening sun. She glanced up at the freshly white painted house and smiled. Finally, they were entering the stage of making this place beautiful again. They all had enough of tearing down and throwing away the old, rotten elements of the house.

But hold on, what's that? The red paint of the small porch pained her eyes. That damn stubborn ass. After all the color-coding and Bree's efforts in persuading him to go for a more gentle looking pale blue, Declan still went ahead with this God-awful vermillion.

Dec needed his head examined. She righted her little black dress and stomped in her high heels over said ugly red porch when Dec opened the door. "And? What do you think?" he smiled a mile wide and opened his arms, showcasing a job he figured well done.

"You never listen, Dec."

She shook her head as she walked up to him. Because if he would really listen to her—or take notice, he'd known how her stomach flip-flopped at the mere sight of his dimples. How her heart skipped a beat at his smiling gray eyes. Damn, she was a mess. She would even put up with this hideous porch if it meant she'd live here with him, waking up every day in those muscular tanned arms.

"Squirt..." he said, and Bree winced at his nickname for her. She wasn't the six-year-old tomboy following him around anymore. In front of Declan stood a twenty-six-year-old who just had an emergency video chat with her sister Gwenn about her outfit tonight.

She was on a mission. The normal 'one-of-the-guys-Bree' wouldn't cut it. Tonight, she wasn't the girl next door and Dec's best friend in her favorite sweater and jeans. No. In front of Declan stood a WO-MAN.

Yes. She emphasized it out loud in her head and his smile faltered. He could always read her mind. So, how he didn't read the signs of her pining and lusting over his Irish ass was the greatest mystery of all times.

Maybe he didn't want to hurt her feelings by addressing it. Or he was afraid to have the same conversation she was about to have with him. Telling him how she felt might ruin their friendship. They both avoided this topic. Well, either way, tonight would be the start of a new chapter in their relationship. Hopefully, a chapter filled with lots of clothes ripping...

"I know, I know..." he said as he held up his hands, making his black stained T-shirt creep up from the top of his dusty jeans. She bit her bottom lip at the sight of his dusty trail of hair going down beneath his belt buckle. Bree cleared her throat.

"The color is gross, Dec. It's—"

"Yeah, I know. You're right. I should have listened to you. But at least for now, it has a coat of paint." He shrugged before he opened his arms for her to step into. She couldn't remember the time he wouldn't invite her into his arms for a hug.

Even wearing a new dress for this special occasion couldn't hold her from hugging his dirty torso. The smell of clean, manly sweat accompanied by wood dust infiltrated her nostrils. She placed her cheek to his T-shirt clad chest to get her fill. He squeezed her tighter for a moment and stepped back to travel his gray eyes over her.

"You seem different. What did I miss? Didn't we talk this morning? What's up?" Declan said as he took her biceps in his calloused hands. The observant cop side of Dec scrutinized her expression as he narrowed his eyes.

"Geez. I'm wearing make-up? Maybe that's it?" Bree said as she tucked a curl behind her ear.

"No. That's not it. It's something *in* your eyes, not *on* your eyes. Your eyes always speak volumes to me. And they're telling me there's something going on you'd rather not say. What's the matter?"

Bree sighed and shook her head. Why was this so hard? He was her best friend; she usually told him everything. Well, perhaps not that she'd masturbated this morning after hanging up the phone with Dec. His raspy voice after he'd just woken up had gotten her all hot and bothered. She'd needed some kind of relief before going into work and had made do with the showerhead.

Oh, how she longed to feel the real deal instead of getting off on just the thought of Declan. They stood so close she could almost taste him. Bree took a deep breath, full of his scent, and closed her eyes for a moment.

Okay, let's do this. It's now or never.

"Dec..." she said as she opened her eyes. His name came out in a pained whisper.

"What is it?"

His eyes searched hers for answers. As he cocked his head, his charcoal longer hair on top swished over his frowned forehead.

She swallowed the big lump in her throat and said, "I'm in love with you."

His brows shot up, and he took a step back from her. His hands let go of her upper arms. Losing his warmth and the lack of a verbal response made her involuntarily shiver. She looked up through her eyelashes and winced at his expression.

Dec rubbed his neck, exposing his hard bicep next to his ear.

A smear of ugly vermillion paint graced his elbow. He shook his head in disbelief.

"Fuck, Squirt. I..."

She swallowed back the tears threatening to overflow her eyelids. After a few hefty blinks, the first damn tears descended. Declan wasted no time and beat her to it as he wiped them away with his thumb.

"Shit..."

He took her cheeks in between the palm of his hands and for a moment; she was sure he would lean in and kiss her. His stormy eyes locked onto hers, but she couldn't read him. How could he control his emotions like this? Didn't she affect him as he did her?

"Say you feel this too, Dec," Bree said. The pleading in her voice was clear.

"I... yes, of course do I love you."

Bree's heart rate went sky high, but his pained stare demolished all hope. And his next words shattered her heart into a thousand pieces.

"But not in that way. I'm sorry, Squirt."

29

EXCERPT DUNCAN - BOOK 1

D UNCAN BOOK 1

SALTY DROPLETS of sweat stung Duncan's eyes as he jabbed his right glove against the cut jaw of his younger brother Ronan. Other than a smothered grunt, the big ape didn't let on Duncan's force affected him.

The grunts of both brothers and the tapping of gloves against each other echoed through the otherwise at this hour deserted gym. A blow to his knee made Duncan swear out loud. Ronan chuckled and said, "Was that as good for you as it was for me?"

Instead of giving in to Ronan's ribbing and losing what's left of his concentration, Duncan danced around Ronan and gave him a high kick to his side. A muffled swear was his only reward and Duncan said, "I don't know, was it?"

He could do cocky too. Duncan hated that he couldn't fight

professionally anymore because of a shoulder injury. Fighting was his life. He was good at it—no, not just good, he was the best. He started Duncan's Dojo with his prize money, and here he was helping the next generation Mills fighter, and Ronan was handing him his ass.

Just in time, Duncan dodged Ronan when he stormed at him, trying to finish their fight on the ground. Because his brother got a few pounds on him and therefore the upper hand in a ground fight, Duncan avoided Ronan's swinging arm as he kept coming at him.

"Stop charging as a bull on steroids, bro. You're wasting energy."

"Don't be such a wuss and stop running from me," Ronan said while stepping into Duncan's reach. Duncan immediately seized the opportunity by giving Ronan a fresh uppercut, but paused his advance when Ronan staggered a few feet backwards.

"We're done for tonight," Duncan said after spitting out his azure custom made mouth guard. He put his sparring glove to his mouth to tear the lace loose between his teeth.

"I ain't done," Ronan said as he narrowed his eyes.

"Yeah, you are. That's what I'm trying to teach you, bro. You've got to keep your focus and stop playing. When you step into—"

"Yeah, yeah. I hear ye," Ronan said in his Irish brogue, meaning it agitated him enough to let the Irish 'ye's' fall from his busted lips. Duncan sighed as he still couldn't get through to him. Annoyed, Duncan threw his second glove over the rope and into his gym bag.

Duncan had to adjust to his new role as coach for the next MMA fighter in the Mills family. Ronan had the necessary physique, since he was even a few inches taller than Duncan's six foot four frame.

And Duncan hated to say, but even after fully recovered from his injury, his brother Ronan still got the stronger arms out of the two. But he'd never tell his cocky arse that. Hell no. The one thing standing in his brother's way of becoming the next Mills champion fighter was his arrogance.

"Let's go to Lucky, bro. I need to find someone to cuddle me arse after that damn uppercut ye threw at me," Ronan said as he trailed after Duncan to the locker rooms. Duncan placed his gym bag on the wooden bench and picked up his towel and shampoo bottle.

"Yeah, I'm down for that," Duncan said. It was already eleven o'clock and after a long day giving classes and sparring with several MMA fighters, he could use some downtime at their family's Irish pub, The Lucky Irishman.

He stepped under the scalding hot spray and closed his eyes, letting the water wash away the remnants of sparring with Ronan. He let his mind go back to the beginning of this year, when Duncan opened his own dojo in an old empty warehouse in the neighborhood of St. Johns in Austin.

His four brothers and his dad had helped him in making the building ready for its new purpose. The demolition and renovation were over in a heartbeat, because all the Mills brothers were built like Duncan—six-foot-four brick walls of muscle.

The dojo was busy with fighters who trained on the fighting mats and in the two boxing rings, and people working out in the fitness area. The yoga and defense classes made for a mixed clientele and gave less of a man cave feel to his dojo. His gym turned out to be a place where all sorts of people could grow and work on themselves. He loved helping people to reach their goals, and he finally started to fit into his new role as a coach to Ronan.

His brother's words brought him back at tonight. Hmm, he could use some cuddling too. It hadn't been that long ago, maybe two days since his last hook-up. But Duncan never went long without a female touch.

Thinking about picking up some random hot piece at their family's Irish pub tonight, brought him to quicken up his pace. He lacked no attention as an MMA fighting champion. Even now as a dojo owner and coach, he still got around.

"You seeing that redhead tonight?" Ronan said as he toweled dried himself on the other side of the locker room.

Ah, he must mean the fiery chick from two nights ago. "No man, you know how it is," Duncan said. "It was fun, but nothing more." He shrugged and stepped into his dark blue jeans. He pulled on a fresh shirt out of his gym bag and slipped on his sneakers. After spraying a not too heavy amount of cologne in his neck, he was ready. Let's see who the flavor of the night would be.

Chapter 2–Kayla

Looking down at the freshly mopped tiles in the grand hall, Kayla shuffled carefully toward the back of the hall where she earlier spotted the elevators. Bumping headfirst into a broad, muscular back cut her cautious shambling short. "Hmpf."

The irritated sound of her victim wasn't lost on Kayla. Taking a quick step back, she apologized. "I'm so sorry. I didn't see you."

At first her eyes drew to a pair of black boots and traveled up a pair of dark blue jeans. When her gaze reached a black T-shirt, she wondered why this man wasn't wearing a coat, as it was only March. She smiled at this observation, as the temperature here in Texas was most definitely different from what she was accustomed to in New Jersey.

"Well now, you're sure getting a real good look."

Oh my God. Was this man for real? He made it sound as if she was ogling him. This guy had some nerve to point that out, even when her eyes still lingered on his broad chest.

She looked up to a chiseled jaw and over to a crooked nose that seemed to have been broken once or twice. His eyes were the lightest green orbs she'd ever seen.

He was easily six foot four with bulky muscles peeping from under the tight sleeves of his black T-shirt. His dark hair was shaved close to his scalp, and if it wouldn't be weird to do to a stranger, she would definitely graze over it with her palm just to feel the smooth, short hairs tickle her palm.

She'd detected the slightest hint of an accent—Irish, maybe? She wasn't sure, but it gave his voice a certain sexiness.

Feeling his gaze upon her, she involuntarily shifted on her favorite black pumps. The twinkling light green eyes looking down at Kayla announced that the lack of enthusiasm she was giving didn't discourage him. No, he studied her as if he was considering her a challenge, his newest conquest even.

"And?" he asked, attempting to keep the conversation going, although it was pretty one sided.

Kayla shook her head, trying to reboot her mind.

"And what?" she asked with a sigh, so over this conversation. She had no time for this; she needed to be at Mills Security in five minutes. Turning her attention to the two elevators, it disappointed Kayla to see that the closest one was on the tenth floor. Great, at least it was moving down. Hopefully, this guy wouldn't go to the same floor as her.

"And do you like what you see?" he clarified, interrupting her thoughts.

"Why? I'd think you wouldn't need any confirmation. Your head is big enough as it is."

Booming laughter followed her statement. It irritated Kayla

that he had the nerve to laugh. The rise of her right brow and a stern look were all she needed to shut him up.

After what had happened over a month ago, she was glad she still had it in her and didn't come across as a pushover. Meeting a man was the last thing on her to-do list.

She needed to be on her A game today and not flirting with some playboy who thought he could have her falling for his, by the look of it, signature panty-dropping smirk.

Kayla had always enjoyed flirting, but she needed no distraction from a tall, muscular, and beautifully rugged man. Yes, she could tell by his stance and attitude, he was definitely a man who was used to getting his way.

He oozed cockiness, a confidence that would normally attract her. But not now, not when her life was upside down and she needed to stay focused.

One of the two elevators passed the sixth floor on its way down to the ground floor, and Kayla intentionally kept her gaze on the doors instead of Mr. Boxer. The name suited him with his crooked nose, scarred right eyebrow, and robust physique.

"Well, I'm wondering if I've lost my touch, as you refuse to even look my way." His tone had lost its playfulness, and Kayla glanced over her shoulder to see if his expression matched his words.

His smirk was gone. Well, at least that was something. And to give him the final blow, Kayla turned back to the elevator doors and continued to ignore him.

The elevator dinged and its doors slid open. After pushing the button with the floor number she needed, she strolled to the back of the elevator and rested her backside at the bar across the fully mirrored elevator. Mr. Boxer prowled across the compact space to stand beside her, his eyes on her the entire time.

The other people in the elevator hastily made room for him.

Why was she still standing there instead of moving when he stood so close to her? Her reaction perplexed her as her skin heated under his gaze and his forwardness when his leg softly touched her thigh as he leaned in to her.

The old Kayla would have given him a chilly stare or a warning threat, which would've sent him running scared out of this elevator, but she couldn't seem to do that just now. Was it because Mr. Boxer intrigued her, or had her recent experiences numbed her?

It disappointed her in herself either way. Hadn't she learned by now that she needed to distance herself from men who looked at her as if they wanted to eat her alive?

"What are you doing?" she said in a loud whisper that had two women in business suits in the elevator looking up from their phones to watch them.

"I'm sorry, but there's not much room in here," he said.

She took a step to her other side, bumping into a bald-headed guy who made a show out of his annoyance by clucking his tongue. Mr. Boxer leaned over Kayla and said, "We got a problem?"

The bald guy swallowed a few times before shaking his head. He didn't answer Mr. Boxer, but by moving himself over to the two women in business suits, he made sure there was no problem.

Kayla dared to look up at Mr. Boxer and he took it as a sign of encouragement as he said, "Let's meet up for drinks tonight."

"No, thank you. I'm not interested." She batted her eyelashes at him before he could sniff out her blatant lie. If she didn't have all this baggage holding her back, she would be very interested to take him up on his offer.

The ding of the elevator interrupted her thoughts. Two office workers entered the elevator, and she looked up to find what floor they were on. She focused on the numbers changing on the display and moved toward the doors.

When Kayla walked out of the elevator, she noticed Mr. Boxer following her in the elevator mirror. It shouldn't surprise her, and it definitely shouldn't give her an extra sway in her step knowing he was walking behind her.

Her four-inch heels clicked on the tiles as she strolled up to the reception desk of Mills Security. A voluptuous brunette in a tight, fitted red dress was typing away at her computer.

The receptionist's chocolate hair was pinned in a knot, but some loose curls bounced next to her hazel eyes. Her red lips pursed into a straight line as she looked up from her computer but didn't give the slightest other acknowledgement of Kayla standing in front of her desk.

"Good morning. My name is Kayla Walsh, and I have a meeting with Donovan Mills."

The brunette's face transformed as she tried for a fake smile. "Good morning, Duncan. How are you? Is Donovan expecting you?"

Kayla looked over her shoulder, and sure enough, Mr. Boxer was standing there smiling at the brunette. What is he smiling at her for? Normally, Kayla would call out the snooty woman for flat-out ignoring her. But she decided against it because she really needed this job.

With everything that'd been going on in the past month, she'd put a dent in her savings account. After recovering for several weeks, she'd had interview after interview this past week now that she no longer had to cover up the bruises.

She'd been getting antsy, often lying awake at night wondering if she could make rent next month. Normally, she could turn to her family for some temporary help, but she couldn't reach out to them. Not yet.

"Hello, Jenna. No, he's not expecting me. As you might have noticed, he's expecting this beautiful lady. Kayla Walsh, was it?"

Kayla hated that Mr. Boxer was acting all chivalrous. He was not supposed to come out of his annoying, flirtatious, manwhore box.

He was supposed to keep irritating her so she could keep up the act of not being affected by him. If she softened toward him, he would get to her. His approach to her up to now told her as much.

"Oh, I'm sorry, I didn't see you there. I'll tell Donovan you're here, but I'm sure that you'll have to wait until he's done meeting with Duncan."

Kayla's smile mirrored Jenna's and for the not-so-observant passerby, it might seem like the two women were being friendly. For Kayla and Jenna, it was clear they would never be friends, not in this lifetime.

She gave Jenna a look that said she was not to be toyed with. "Yes, please call him and let him know I'm ready for him."

Jenna's eyes narrowed, shooting daggers at her. To make matters worse, Duncan muttered that he was "over this shit" and walked toward an office door, which Kayla assumed was Donovan's.

"Duncan! Wait! You can't go in there. I have to call Donovan first to—"

Before Jenna could finish her sentence, Duncan opened the dark wooden office door without knocking.

It gave Kayla an unobstructed view of a tall, built man in a tailored suit with raven hair who stepped out of his embrace with a woman with straight strawberry blonde hair. He looked so similar to Duncan that Kayla was sure the men had to be related.

The woman was wearing a tight black minidress with black

pumps, the kind with a red surface underneath. She wore impeccable makeup and a diamond bracelet with a matching necklace. Even if she was a little flushed, the woman maintained a certain air about her to show being interrupted during her rendezvous didn't faze her.

Jenna gasped in shock behind Kayla. "I've had enough of this! I quit!" She turned and stormed to her reception desk to pull out the bottom drawer. Jenna took out her purse, which she slung in a determined swing over her shoulder as she strode off toward the elevators.

"Duncan, ever heard of knocking?" Donovan held his head up high and his shoulders straight. Donovan Mills was unapologetic in his attitude, as was the strawberry blonde next to him, her eyes pinned on Kayla.

"Don, that makes number three this month. Why is it so hard for you to behave and not scare away your assistants?" Duncan said while looking over his shoulder at Jenna, who was pushing the elevator button multiple times, as if that would make the elevator come sooner.

"Dunc, I think it's more that she's disappointed she didn't get a taste of me," Donovan said while readjusting his cufflinks. He then straightened his tie and looked at Duncan as if to say now that he'd handled the loose ends, he was ready to proceed with his day.

"Hmmm, and it's quite the taste," Strawberry purred next to the mahogany desk which Donovan was now leaning against. Duncan groaned, and Kayla rolled her eyes at her statement.

"And that is your cue to leave us," Donovan said in an even voice. The woman looked up at Donovan and tried to pout her lips, but before she could do so, Donovan put his index finger over her mouth.

"Shhh. No need to drag this out. We had our fun, and now it's time for you to leave."

As if hypnotized, she nodded at Donovan and sauntered toward the door.

"Keep in touch?" the woman asked as she looked hopefully over her shoulder at Donovan. When he didn't answer, her shoulders sagged a bit, but she kept on moving toward the elevators.

Entering the office, Kayla turned and looked around. It was a corner office with a full view of downtown Austin where the sun reflected in the blue-glass exterior of the Frost Bank Tower. In the left corner stood a black leather couch, a coffee table, and some filing cabinets, but what caught her eye were the multiple paintings hanging on the wall. They seemed expressive with dark coloring and abstract figures.

"Do you like my paintings? I'd love to make one of you." Kayla noticed the tension coming from Duncan at this statement from Donovan.

His jaw set tight, he narrowed his eyes at him. Donovan was an attractive man, but in a different kind of way than Duncan. Donovan oozed authority and sex, but he had something dark about him she couldn't pinpoint.

He resembled Duncan if you ignored the wavy inky hair, but he was an unattainable version of him.

Even though she'd just met Duncan ten minutes ago, she had no doubt that he was a player. But he seemed accessible, and he had a certain playful, roguish air about him she found attractive.

Kayla enjoyed butting heads with her former partners, joking around and teasing each other. She most definitely didn't get the teasing vibe from Donovan. No, he was not the joking-around type. He was in control and made sure everyone knew it.

"That will never happen, Don." Duncan strode across the office and stood next to Kayla, who in return took a few steps aside so she stood at an arm's length from him.

Duncan sighed, and when she looked in his mint green eyes, she was a little stunned by his serious expression.

He looked straight back at Kayla as he said, "She is not one of your playthings. Forget it, bro."

ALSO BY ANNA CASTOR

The Lucky Irish series:

ABOUT THE AUTHOR

Anna
Castor

Anna loves to write heartfelt and steamy romance series. She falls in love with her characters as they go through their ups and downs. Anna often laughs out loud behind her laptop as she writes the banter between siblings. Sometimes, she cries as a result from the real talk that comes with family. There's no hiding from a nosy Pops ;-) Her books are for mature readers only because of their steamy content.

Anna Castor lives in a small town near Amsterdam, The Netherlands, with her husband and their three young daughters. When she's not writing and has some time left between bringing her kids to school and picking them up from play dates or volleyball practice, she's glued to her e-reader.

Anna is a former wedding photographer turned author. While photographing weddings, Anna loved being a part of the couple's special day to tell their (love) story through her pictures. Each wedding had a different story to tell: the histories of the bride and groom, their family dynamics, their challenges in life, and of course, how they met and fell in love.

And now Anna takes her readers through the troubles and hardships her characters may come across on their journey to a happily ever after.

Anna loves to hear from her readers <3. Follow her online to get updates on new releases, ARC opportunities, freebies and more!

Connect with her online:
Website: www.annacastor.com
Newsletter: www.annacastor.com/subscribe

ACKNOWLEDGMENTS

A huge thank you to all of the amazing readers out there who took a chance on reading one of my books! It means the world to me that you enjoy the characters like I do. Some even fell in love with the series and I'm happy to keep popping out Lucky Irish books for you! :)

Thank you, Tiffany Grimes from Burgeon Design and Editorial, for working with me on the third book of the series. It was such a pleasure working with you. You've helped me to bring out more sides to Errin and Brennan and how to work on several points to improve my writing. I'm so happy that I've found you!

To Hakima, my dear friend who always speaks her mind. From hilarious outbursts to confrontational remarks, it's never a dull moment with you! I love how you stay true to your spirit and bring so much laughter and happiness to our lives.

To my family, my husband and three daughters, you give me so much inspiration on writing about love and strong-willed heroines in particular. Every day, you make me feel so loved, and I can only hope that I'm making you proud.